Is there anything sexier than a hot cowboy?

How about 4 of them!

New York Times bestselling author
Vicki Lewis Thompson is back in the Blaze 2013 lineup,
and this year she's offering her readers *even more*....

Sons of Chance

Chance isn't just the last name of these
rugged Wyoming cowboys—it's their motto, too!

Saddle up with

#751 *I CROSS MY HEART*
(June)

#755 *WILD AT HEART*
(July)

#759 *THE HEART WON'T LIE*
(August)

And the first full-length
Sons of Chance Christmas story

#775 *COWBOYS & ANGELS*
(December)

Take a chance...on a Chance!

Dear Reader,

We learned in school that Benjamin Franklin's preferred candidate for the United States of America's national bird was the wild turkey. I've seen wild turkeys and I've seen bald eagles, and with all due respect to Benny, he was full of it on this subject. Wild turkeys are cool in their own way, but I've never seen one soar. Eagles have soaring down pat, and that's what inspires us.

Consequently, I lived out another of my fantasy lives with Naomi Perkins, who's spending her summer in Wyoming on an observation platform watching a nest of bald eagles. Those smart eagles built their nest on Last Chance property, which turns out to be a very good thing for Naomi for several reasons. Chief among those is Luke Griffin, a new hire at the ranch who's as fascinated by eagles as I am. He's also fascinated by a woman who will gladly forgo modern conveniences in order to camp out and study wildlife.

Welcome to another Sons of Chance story! Turns out those cowboys keep riding into my imagination, and then some feisty woman shows up, and you know how much fun that can be! So come along with me for another visit to the Last Chance Ranch. Your friends are all there waiting for you!

Soaringly yours,

Vicki Lewis Thompson

Vicki Lewis Thompson

Wild at Heart

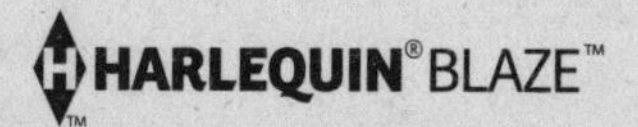

ISBN-13: 978-0-373-79759-2

WILD AT HEART

This edition published by arrangement with Harlequin Books S.A.

For questions and comments about the quality of this book, please contact us at CustomerService@Harlequin.com.

HARLEQUIN®
www.Harlequin.com

Printed in U.S.A.

ABOUT THE AUTHOR

New York Times bestselling author Vicki Lewis Thompson's love affair with cowboys started with the Lone Ranger, continued through Maverick and took a turn south of the border with Zorro. She views cowboys as the Western version of knights in shining armor—rugged men who value honor, honesty and hard work. Fortunately for her, she lives in the Arizona desert, where broad-shouldered, lean-hipped cowboys abound. Blessed with such an abundance of inspiration, she only hopes that she can do them justice. Visit her website, www.vickilewisthompson.com.

Books by Vicki Lewis Thompson

HARLEQUIN BLAZE

544—WANTED!*
550—AMBUSHED!*
556—CLAIMED!*
618—SHOULD'VE BEEN A COWBOY*
624—COWBOY UP*
630—COWBOYS LIKE US*
651—MERRY CHRISTMAS, BABY*
"It's Christmas, Cowboy!"
687—LONG ROAD HOME*
693—LEAD ME HOME*
699—FEELS LIKE HOME*
751—I CROSS MY HEART*

*Sons of Chance

To the dedicated folks who devote endless hours
and abandon creature comforts so that
our precious wildlife is protected. Thank you!

Prologue

July 3, 1984, Last Chance Ranch

ON PRINCIPLE, ARCHIBALD CHANCE approved of getting the ranch house gussied up for the Independence Day festivities. He was as patriotic as the next man. But the excitement of an impending party had transformed his usually well-behaved grandsons into wild things. From his position on a ladder at the far end of the porch, he could hear all three of them tearing around inside. He hoped to get the red, white and blue streamers tacked up before any of them came out.

That hope died as the screen door banged open and a bundle of two-year-old energy with a fistful of small flags raced down the porch toward him. The kid was more interested in who was coming after him than looking where he was going. A tornado in tiny cowboy boots.

"Nicky!" The screen door banged again as Sarah, Archie's daughter-in-law, dashed after him.

Giggling, Nicky put his head down and ran as fast as

his little legs would carry him. With no time to climb down, Archie dropped the bunting, tossed the nails into the coffee can and braced himself against the ladder as he shouted a warning.

Fortunately Sarah was quick. She scooped up both boy and flags a split second before he smashed into the ladder. "Those are for the table, young man."

"I gots flags, Mommy!" the little boy crowed.

"Yes, and they have pointy ends. Don't run with them, Nicholas." Sarah glanced up at Archie. "Sorry about that."

"Gabe gots flags, too!" Nicky announced.

Sarah wheeled around, and sure enough, there was little Gabe, not yet two, motoring toward them with a flag in each hand.

"I wager somebody's supplying them with those," Archie said.

"Yes, I wager you're right. And his name is Jack. Excuse me, Archie. I have a five-year-old who needs a reminder about the dangers of giving pointy objects to little boys." Confiscating the flags from both toddlers amid wails of distress, she herded them back inside.

"You're doing a great job, Sarah!" Archie called after her. He never missed an opportunity to tell her that. She'd given birth to only one of those kids, baby Gabriel, and she'd inherited the other two as part of the deal for being willing to marry Jonathan Chance. She loved all three kids equally, and she loved their father with the kind of devotion that made Archie's heart swell with gratitude.

As he turned back to his bunting chore, the screen

door squeaked again, signaling another interruption. He'd oil those hinges today. He hadn't realized how bad they were.

Glancing toward the door, he smiled. This was the kind of interruption he appreciated.

Nelsie approached with two glasses of iced tea. "Time for a break, Arch."

"Don't mind if I do." Hooking the hammer in his belt, he carried the coffee can full of nails in the crook of his arm as he descended the ladder to join his wife. "How're things going in there?"

"Not too bad, considering. I'm glad we decided to host the after-parade barbecue this year, but we didn't factor in the dynamics of having both babies able to walk and Jack putting them up to all manner of things. They'll do anything he tells them, especially Nicky."

Archie put down the hammer and nails before accepting a glass of tea and settling into the rocking chair next to her. They'd bought several rockers to line the porch, which would come in mighty handy during the barbecue. "Those boys are a handful, all right." He took a sip of tea. "Wouldn't trade 'em for all the tea in China, though."

"Me, either, the little devils." Nelsie chuckled. "Oh, you know what? I saw a bald eagle fly over early this morning. Forgot to tell you that."

"Huh. Wonder if there's a nest somewhere."

"Could be. Anyway, I thought it was appropriate, a bald eagle showing up so close to the Fourth. Maybe he, or she, will do a flyover tomorrow for our guests."

"I'll see if I can arrange it for you."

She smiled at him in that special way that only Nelsie could smile. “If you could, I believe you’d do it, Archie.”

“Yep, that’s a fact.” They’d celebrated their forty-seventh anniversary last month, and he loved this woman more every day. He would do anything for her. And to his amazement, she would do anything for him, too.

He was one lucky cuss, and he knew it. His father used to say that Chance men were lucky when it counted. In Archie’s view, finding a woman like Nelsie counted for a whole hell of a lot.

1

Present Day

FROM A PLATFORM twenty feet in the air, Naomi Perkins focused her binoculars on a pair of fuzzy heads sticking out of a gigantic nest across the clearing. Those baby eagles sure had the cuteness factor going on. If they lived to adulthood, they'd grow into majestic birds of prey, but at this stage they were achingly vulnerable.

Blake Scranton, the university professor who'd hired her to study the nestlings, was an infirm old guy who was writing a paper on Jackson Hole bald-eagle nesting behavior. He expected her firsthand observations to be the centerpiece of his paper, which would bring more attention to the eagle population in the area and should also give a boost to ecotourism.

Lowering her binoculars, she crouched down to check the battery reading of the webcam mounted on the observation-platform railing. Still plenty of juice.

As she glanced up, a movement caught her eye. A rider had appeared at the edge of the clearing.

In the week she'd spent monitoring this nest on the far boundary of the Last Chance Ranch, she'd seen plenty of four-legged animals, but none of the two-legged variety until now. Standing, she trained her binoculars on the rider and adjusted the focus. Then she sucked in a breath of pure feminine appreciation. A superhot cowboy was headed in her direction.

She didn't recognize him. He wasn't one of the Chance brothers or any of their longtime ranch hands. Her eight-by-eight platform, tucked firmly into the branches of a tall pine, allowed her to watch him unobserved.

If he looked up, he might notice the platform even though it was semicamouflaged. But he was too far away to see her. Her tan shirt and khaki shorts would blend into the shadows.

Still, she'd be less visible if she sat down. Easing slowly to the deck, she propped her elbows on the two-foot railing designed to keep her from falling off. Then she refocused her binoculars and began a top-to-bottom inventory.

He wore his hair, which was mostly covered by his hat, on the longish side. From here it looked dark but not quite black. She liked the retro effect of collar-length hair, which hinted at the possibility that the guy was a little less civilized than your average male.

The brim of his hat blocked her view of his eyes. She decided to think of them as brown, because she had a preference for dark-haired men with brown eyes.

He had a strong jaw and a mouth bracketed by smile lines. So maybe he had a sense of humor.

Moving on, she took note of broad shoulders that gave him a solid, commanding presence. He sat tall in the saddle but without any tension, as if he took a relaxed approach to life.

Thanking the German makers of her binoculars for their precision, she gazed at the steady rise and fall of his powerful chest. He'd left a couple of snaps undone in deference to the heat, and that was enough to reveal a soft swirl of dark chest hair. Vaguely she realized she'd crossed the line from observing to ogling, but no one would ever have to know.

Next she focused on his slim hips and the easy way his denim-clad thighs gripped the Western saddle. While she was in the vicinity, she checked out his package. She had to own that impulse. If she ever caught some guy giving her such a thorough inspection, she'd be insulted.

But she didn't intend to get caught, or even be seen. After a solid week of camping, she was far too bedraggled to chat with a guy, especially a guy who looked like this one. He was the sort of cowboy she'd want to meet at the Spirits and Spurs when she looked smokin' hot in a tight pair of jeans, a low-cut blouse and her red dancing boots.

He could be a visitor out for a trail ride, but if he was a ranch hand, he might come into town for a beer on Saturday nights. She'd ask around—subtly, of course. He'd be well worth the effort of climbing out of this tree and sprucing up a bit.

She was due for some fun of the male variety, come to think of it. She'd been celibate since… Had it really been almost a year since Arnold? And that hadn't been a particularly exciting relationship, now that she had some distance and could look at it objectively.

She had a bad tendency to set her sights too low, which was how she'd ended up in bed with Arnold, a fellow researcher in a Florida wildlife program. If she should by some twist of fate end up in bed with this cowboy, she could never say her sights were set too low. He was breathtaking.

He was also getting too close for her to continue ogling. She regretfully lowered her binoculars and eased back from the edge of the platform. If she scooted up against the tree trunk, he'd never know she was there.

Emmett Sterling, the ranch foreman, and Jack, the oldest of the Chance brothers, had built the platform for her. They'd also mentioned her presence to the cowhands so they'd be aware in case they rode out this way. But even if the rider had noticed the structure, he'd have no idea whether it was currently occupied.

She could be doing any number of things. She might be hiking back to town for supplies or taking a nap in the dome tent she'd pitched down near the stream that ran along the Last Chance's northern boundary. Leaning against the tree, she listened to the steady clop-clop of hooves approaching.

She needed to sneeze. Of course. People always needed to sneeze when they were trying to hide. She pressed her finger against the base of her nose.

Finally the urge to sneeze went away, but she felt a tickle in her throat. *Clop, clop, clop, clop.* The horse and rider sounded as if they were only a few yards from her tree. She needed to cough. She really did. Maybe if she was extremely careful and exceptionally quiet, she could pick up her energy drink and take a sip.

Usually while she was up here, the songbirds chirped merrily in the branches around her and the breeze made a nice sighing sound. That kind of ambient noise would be welcome so she could take a drink of her favorite bright green beverage without danger of detection. But the air was completely still and even the birds seemed to have taken an intermission.

The horse snorted. They were *very* close. If only the horse would snort again, she could coordinate her swallow with that. She raised the bottle to her mouth but was greeted by absolute silence.

That means he's stopped right under your tree, idiot. Adrenaline pumped through her as she held her breath and fought the urge to cough.

"Anybody up there?"

His unexpected question made her jump. She lost her grip on the bottle, which rolled to the edge of the platform and toppled off.

The horse spooked and the man cursed. So did Naomi. So much for going unnoticed.

The horse settled down, but the man continued to swear. "What *is* this damned sticky crap, anyway?"

Filled with foreboding, she crawled to the edge of the platform and peered down. Her gorgeous cowboy had taken a direct hit from her energy drink. He yanked off his hat, causing green liquid that had been caught in the brim to run down the front of his shirt. "Oh, *God.* I've been slimed!"

"Sorry."

He glanced up at her. "You must be Naomi Perkins."

"I am." Even from twenty feet away, or more like ten or twelve since he was still on his horse, she could see that he was royally pissed. "And you are?"

"Luke Griffin."

"Sorry about dousing you, Luke."

"I'll wash, and my clothes will wash, but the hat… And it's my best hat, too."

"I'll have it cleaned for you." She wondered why he'd worn his best hat out on the trail. Usually cowboys saved their best for special occasions.

Blowing out a breath, he surveyed the damage. "That's okay. Maybe Sarah can work some magic on it."

"Sarah Chance?"

"Right. The boss lady."

So he was a ranch hand. "She might be able to clean it." Naomi, who'd grown up in this area, had great respect for Sarah, widow of Jonathan and co-owner of the ranch along with her three sons. If anybody could salvage a hat covered with energy drink, Sarah could.

"What's in that stuff, so I can tell her what to use on it?"

"Oh, you know. Glucose, electrolytes, vegetable juice. I think it's the broccoli that turns it green. Or maybe it's the liquefied spinach."

He grimaced. "That sounds nasty."

"I don't always eat three squares while I'm working, so the energy drink helps me stay nourished and hydrated."

"You must be really dedicated if you can stomach that on a regular basis."

She shrugged. "You get used to it."

"You might. I wouldn't."

"So are you out here checking the fence?"

He hooked his damaged hat on the saddle horn and gazed up at her. "Actually, I rode out to see how you were getting along."

"You did?" That surprised her. "Did Emmett send you?"

"Not exactly. But he told us what you were trying to accomplish—documenting nesting behavior for a professor who plans to write up a paper on it. I thought that sounded like interesting work. I had a little spare time, so I decided to find out if you're okay."

"That's thoughtful." Especially when he didn't know her from Adam. Nor did she know him, although under different circumstances, she'd be happy to get acquainted. "I'm doing fine, thanks."

"How about the eagle babies? Are they all right?"

"So far." Apparently he was curious about the eagles. She could understand that. They were fascinating creatures.

"Good. That's good." A fly started buzzing around him, followed by a couple of bees. He waved them away. "They're after the sweet smell, I guess."

"I'm sure." He'd probably hoped to visit her platform and get a bird's-eye view of the eagles. Time to stop being vain and let him do that. "Listen, did you want to come up and take a look at the nest?"

"I'd love to, but I'm all sticky and attracting bugs."

"So maybe you could wash some of it off in the stream."

"Yeah, that might work."

"I'll come down. I know the best spot along the bank for washing up."

He smiled. "I'd like that. Thanks."

"Be right there." Wow, that was some smile he had going on. It almost made her forget that she looked like something the cat dragged in. She'd read that first impressions carried a tremendous amount of weight. As she started down the rope ladder, she hoped he'd make allowances.

DESPITE HAVING BEEN drenched in sticky, sweet green stuff, Luke wanted a look at Naomi Perkins. He hoped she'd be worth the possibility that he'd ruined his best hat. Had he known she possessed a hair-trigger startle response, he would have called out to her long before he'd reached her tree.

But as he'd approached, he'd assumed the platform was deserted. That was the only explanation for the total silence that had greeted him. If she'd been there, he'd reasoned, *she* would have greeted *him.*

That was the accepted way out here in the West. When a person laid claim to a portion of the great outdoors, be it with a campfire or a platform in a tree, they welcomed incoming riders. He was an incoming rider. She had to have noticed him. Yet for some reason she'd played possum.

So it was with great interest that he watched her climb down the rope ladder. First appeared a serviceable pair of hiking boots. He might have figured that.

Then came… Sweet Lord, she had an ass worthy of an exotic dancer. A man could forgive a whole bucket of that green glop landing on him for a chance to watch Naomi Perkins descend a ladder. He no longer cared about the sad condition of his hat, even though that Stetson had set him back a considerable amount of money.

She wore her tan T-shirt pulled out, not tucked in, but even so, he could tell that her slender waist did credit to the rest of her. Her breasts shifted invitingly as she descended, and by the time she'd reached the ground, he was glad he'd ridden out here.

Besides looking good coming down the ladder, she'd accomplished the climb with dexterity. She seemed perfectly at home out here by herself. He admired that kind of self-sufficiency. He'd guessed she might be that type of woman from the moment Emmett had described the job she was doing.

She'd put her honey-blond hair up in a careless ponytail. He could hardly expect some elaborate style from someone who'd been camping for days. Then she turned around, and he was lost.

Eyes bluer than morning glories, a heart-shaped face and pink lips that formed a perfect Cupid's bow. He'd never thought about his ideal woman, but from the fierce pounding of his heart, he suspected he was looking at her.

Before coming to the Jackson Hole area to work at the Last Chance eight months ago, he'd spent a couple of years in Sacramento. Although that city wasn't Hollywood by any means, he'd met plenty of women, young and old, who subscribed to plastic surgery and Botox beauty regimes. And the makeup—they wouldn't walk out the door without it. Some slept in it.

Standing before him was someone who wore not an ounce of makeup. She had an expressive face that obviously hadn't been nipped and tucked. In her khaki shorts and tan shirt, she seemed ready for adventure, like a sidekick for Indiana Jones. He didn't run across women like Naomi all that often. He felt like hoisting this treasure up onto his saddle and riding off with her into the sunset.

Not literally, of course. Sunset wasn't for several hours. Besides, that dramatic gesture sounded good in theory, but in reality he wasn't a good candidate for riding into the sunset with a woman on his horse. That implied that he'd made some pretty big promises to her.

He was a rolling stone who didn't make those kinds of promises. He traveled light. Even so, he wouldn't mind spending some time with the luscious Miss Perkins when she wasn't busy watching eagles.

Now that she was on the ground, he dismounted. "I'd shake your hand, but I'm afraid we'd be stuck together for eternity. My hands are covered with that green stuff."

"Understood."

He waved away more flies. "Time to get it off. Thanks for coming down to keep me company." Leading his horse, he started toward the stream a few yards away.

"It's the least I could do." She fell into step beside him. Their boots crunched the pine needles underfoot and sent up a sharp, clean scent that helped counteract the sweetness of the energy drink.

"Your folks own the Shoshone Diner, right?" he asked.

"Yes."

"I like the food there."

"Me, too. Now you're making me hungry for my mom's meat loaf."

"I would be, too, if I'd been trying to survive on that green junk. Listen, I didn't mean to scare you by calling to you just now. I thought nobody was up there, but I wanted to make sure." He glanced over at her to see what she might have to say for herself on that score.

Her cheeks turned pink. "I didn't realize you'd come out here because of the eagles. I assumed you'd ride on by."

"You didn't think someone riding by would stop and say howdy?"

"Sure, if they knew I was up there."

"So you were hiding from me?"

She nodded.

"Why?" He had a terrible thought. "Did you think I might hurt you?"

"No. I'm used to taking care of myself. I have bear spray and I know karate."

"I'm glad to hear it." It was the way he'd imagined she would be, resourceful and ready for anything. Very attractive traits. "But it doesn't explain why you were hiding."

She gestured to her herself and laughed. "Because I'm a hot mess!"

"You are?" He stared at her in confusion, unable to figure out what she meant.

"Okay, now you're just being nice, and I appreciate it, but I've been out here for a week. I've slept in a tent, washed up in the stream and put on clothes that were stuffed in a backpack. And then there's my hair."

"Okay, your hair might be sort of supercasual." He reached over, pulled a twig out of her ponytail and dropped it to the ground. "But the rest of you is just fine." He didn't know her well enough to tell her she looked sexy as hell. Her rumpled, accessible presentation worked for him way better than a slinky outfit. He related to someone who could survive without modern conveniences.

"Supercasual." She chuckled. "That's a great euphemism for *trashed.*"

"I've seen celebrities whose hair looked way worse than yours, and it was fixed like that on purpose."

"What a gentlemanly thing to say." She pointed through the trees. "Right over there is a nice sandy spot. It's where I go in."

"Perfect." When he reached the bank of the creek, he let Smudge, the Last Chance gelding he usually rode, have a drink.

She came to stand beside him. "You're right, Luke. I overreacted to the idea of having company."

"I'm surprised you'd be so embarrassed." He finished watering the horse, backed him up and dropped the reins to ground-tie him. Then he turned toward Naomi. "Like I said, you look fine to me."

"I wouldn't have been embarrassed if Emmett had come out, or Jack. But I'd never met you." She shrugged. "I guess the vanity thing kicked in."

He gazed at her. "How did you know I wasn't Emmett or Jack?" Then he realized she must have binoculars. "Oh. You were spying on me."

Her blush deepened, giving her away.

Gradually he began to understand the issue. She'd used her binoculars to identify the person riding toward her lookout spot, which was natural. But when she'd discovered he was a stranger, she'd worried about making a bad impression. That was flattering.

"If it makes you feel any better," he said, "I wore my best hat out here on purpose. I wanted to make a good impression on you."

"You did? Why?"

"Well..." He started unsnapping his sticky shirt, starting with the cuffs on his sleeves. "I've been hearing a lot about you."

"Like what?"

"Oh, that you were this cute blonde who'd just moved back home after doing wildlife research for the state of Florida. They said you wrestled alligators and captured pythons and such." He unfastened the snaps running down the front of his shirt and pulled the tail out of his jeans. He felt her gaze on him. Well, that was okay. He wasn't ashamed of his body.

She seemed to get a kick out of the talk about her, though. "You'll have to forgive people for exaggerating," she said with a smile. "I didn't wrestle alligators. Sometimes I had to snare them and move them away from populated areas. But I never dealt with a python by myself."

"Even so, here you are out in the wilderness studying a nest of eagles. In my book, that makes you unusual."

"Sorry to disappoint you, but I'm not that exciting."

"I'm not disappointed at all. I'd have been disappointed to come out here and find you using a battery-powered hair dryer and painting your nails." If she was paying attention, she'd figure out he was attracted to her outdoor lifestyle.

"Thank you. I appreciate your saying that."

"On the other hand, I'm sure I failed to make a good impression on you, swearing and carrying on like I did. Sorry about that." He stripped off his shirt and wadded it up in preparation for dunking it in the water.

"No need to be sorry. I would've reacted the same way if I'd been showered with sticky green stuff."

Something in her voice made him pause and glance at her. To his delight, she was looking at him with a definite gleam in her eye. When he caught her at it, she blushed and turned away.

All righty, then. It appeared that taking off his shirt had been a very good idea.

2

If Naomi had realized that spilling her energy drink would make Luke take off his shirt, she would have done it on purpose. Pecs and abs like his belonged in a calendar. And unlike the shaved versions featured in muscle-building magazines, Luke had manly chest hair that highlighted his flat nipples and traced a path to the metal edge of his belt buckle.

But he'd caught her looking. He hadn't seemed to mind. In fact, she'd spotted a flicker of amusement in his eyes, which were, thank you, God, velvet brown.

"I'll go rinse this out."

"Good idea." Now, there was an idiotic response. Rinsing out his shirt wasn't merely a *good* idea. It was the *whole* idea, the reason they'd walked to the stream in the first place.

She watched him kneel on the embankment and dunk his shirt in the water. The stream wasn't large, no more than fifteen feet across at its widest point, but it ran deep enough in spots for fish to thrive, which was why the eagles were nesting here.

But she wasn't thinking about eagles now. Instead she gazed at the broad, muscled back of Luke Griffin and wondered what it would be like to feel those muscles move under her palms. Having such thoughts about a virtual stranger wasn't like her.

Except he didn't feel like a stranger. He'd come out here because of an interest in the eagles and curiosity about the woman studying them. Instead of being turned off by her rumpled appearance, he seemed to prefer it. That made him the sort of man she'd like to get to know.

At first he'd been understandably upset about getting doused with the energy drink, but apparently he was a good-natured sort of guy who rolled with the punches. Anyone would think he'd had to wash out his clothes in a stream numerous times from the efficiency with which he swirled the shirt in the water and wrung it out.

Then he set it on a nearby rock. Reaching into his back pocket, he pulled out a blue bandanna and plunged it into the water before rubbing his face, chest and shoulders with it.

Naomi felt like a voyeur standing there while he washed up. She could offer to help, but she wasn't sure that was appropriate, either. What could she do, wash his back?

At last he stood, his dripping shirt in one hand and his soaked bandanna in the other. "I'm considering whether I should put my hat in the water or not."

"I can't advise you." Wow, he was beautiful. She had a tough time remembering her name while he faced her, his chest glistening with droplets of water. Evaluating the best procedure for cleaning his hat was beyond her mental capabilities at the moment.

"I'm doing it. It can't get any worse." He walked toward her with the shirt and the bandanna. "Maybe you could find a tree branch for these."

"Sure." She took them, although she wondered what his plan might be. Hanging something to dry implied sticking around awhile. Was that what he had in mind?

Maybe he only wanted his shirt to get dry enough that it wouldn't feel clammy when he put it on, but that would take more than ten minutes. Fine with her. She wouldn't mind spending more time with this sexy cowboy. She found a fairly level branch for both the shirt and the bandanna. As a veteran camper, she was used to such maneuvers.

As she finished hanging up his stuff, he came back holding his saturated hat. "At least it won't attract flies on the way home." He looked around, found a convenient twig sticking out of a tree trunk and hung his hat on it. "I need the bandanna back. One more chore." Grabbing it, he returned to the stream and soaked the bandanna.

Naomi wasn't sure what his goal was until he walked over to his horse and started wiping its neck. Apparently the energy drink had anointed the brown-and-white paint, too. She gave Luke points for wanting to get the stuff off to keep the animal from being pestered by flies, as well.

His considerate gesture also provided her with quite a show. She wondered if he had any idea how his muscles rippled in the dappled sunlight while he worked on that horse. If she could have taken a video, it would be an instant hit on YouTube—gorgeous guy demonstrates his love of animals. What could be sweeter?

Finally he rinsed out the bandanna again and returned it to the branch where his shirt hung. "I think that takes care of the worst of it."

"You're causing me to rethink my consumption of energy drinks. I never dreamed one little bottle could create such a disaster."

He smiled at her. "Ah, it wasn't so bad. The cold water feels good."

"I know it does. That stream was a lifesaver this week when the temperatures kicked up."

"I'll bet. Now that you mention it, you look a little flushed. You can use my bandanna if you—" He paused and chuckled. "Never mind. You probably don't want to rinse your face with the bandanna I just used on my horse."

"I wouldn't care about that. But don't worry about me. I'm used to being hot."

His sudden laughter made the brown-and-white paint lift his head and stare at them. "I'm not touching that line."

"Oh, dear God." She felt a new blush coming on. "I didn't mean it like that." But he'd taken it like that. To her surprise, this beautiful shirtless cowboy was flirting with her. What a rush.

"Now you really look as if you could use a splash of cold water."

"It's my blond coloring. I blush at the drop of a hat." Or the drop of a shirt.

"It looks good on you." He gazed at her with warmth in his brown eyes.

She felt that warmth in every cell of her body, causing her to think of truly crazy things, like what it would be like to kiss him. She'd actually moved a step closer when the piercing cry of an eagle grabbed her attention.

Breaking eye contact, she looked up through the trees and saw the female sail overhead, a fish in her talons.

"Wow." Luke stared after the departing eagle. "He's huge."

"She."

He glanced at Naomi. "She? You mean her mate is even bigger than that?"

"No, her mate is smaller. Female eagles are bigger than the males." After a week of observation, Naomi could distinguish the female's eight-foot wingspan from that of her smaller mate.

"Well, blow me down with a feather. I didn't know that."

"Many people don't. They think any male creature is automatically bigger than the female, but that's not universally true."

He grinned at her. "You said that with a certain amount of relish."

"Maybe." She returned his smile. "It's fun to smash

stereotypes. By the way, did you happen to notice what kind of fish she had?"

"Looked like a trout to me."

"I thought so, too. I have to go back up and document the feeding time and the type of food on my computer. As I said, you're welcome to come up and check out the nest."

"I'd love to." He sounded eager. "But not if I'll get in your way. Or break the platform."

"You won't. Emmett and Jack were both up there together, testing its strength. They made sure it was sturdy."

"In that case, lead the way."

She walked quickly back to the tree. "This ladder will hold you, too. But we can't be on it at the same time." She started up.

"I'll wait until you give me the okay."

Climbing the dangling ladder was much easier than going down, and she made the trip in no time. "All clear. Come on up." She stood, glanced around her little research area and wondered what he'd think of it.

He hoisted himself up on the platform with another display of muscle. "What a view! Makes me want to be an eagle."

Funny, but she could almost imagine that. He had the alert gaze and restrained power she associated with eagles and hawks. "Not me. Flying would be cool, but I wouldn't like living without a roof over my head."

"I could live with that in return for the freedom of being able to fly anytime I felt like it. Yeah, the life of an eagle would suit me just fine." His glance took in the trappings of her work—the webcam mounted to the railing, the camp stool and small folding table for her laptop, her camera bag and a small cooler for her snacks and energy drinks. "Cozy setup."

"Thanks." It felt a lot cozier with him in it. At five-four, she didn't take up much room, so the area had seemed plenty large enough. Now she wondered how she'd be able to move around without bumping into him.

"Aren't you supposed to be recording stuff?"

Yes, she was, and his bare chest had distracted her from her duties. "Right." She picked up her binoculars and handed them to him. "You can help. Do you see the nest?"

"Sure do. From up here it's hard to miss." He raised the binoculars. "Big old thing, isn't it? Wow! There they are, two baby eagles getting lunch from Mom. That's impressive."

"See if you can keep track of whether one's getting more than the other." She sat down and turned on her laptop. "One of the nestlings is bigger and I suspect it's getting more food."

"That's what it looks like." Luke stood facing the clearing, booted feet spread. He looked like a captain at the helm of his ship as he studied the nest through the binoculars. "Look at that! Shoving the other one out of the way. Hey, you, you're supposed to share!"

Naomi smiled. She'd had the same thoughts, but hearing them come out of Luke's mouth made her realize how silly they were. Wildlife researchers couldn't afford to anthropomorphize their subjects. Giving them human attributes might work for Disney, but not for science.

Speaking of science, she'd better start making notes instead of watching Luke watch the eagles.

"Here comes the dad."

Yikes. She'd completely missed seeing the male eagle fly overhead. "If you'll describe what's happening, I'll just take down what you dictate."

"He came in with another fish, and that's definitely a trout. I think we're safe to say they're having trout for lunch. Now Mom's flown off and Dad's feeding the kids. Damned if that bigger baby isn't getting more of the second course, too."

"It happens. I'll bet you've seen it with puppies and kittens. They compete for the food. The most aggressive ones get the most food."

"Yeah, but when that happened with a litter my dog had, I supplemented so the runt didn't die."

She gave him points for that, too. "But these are wild creatures. If you tried to interfere, the parents might abandon both of them. I wouldn't worry too much. There are only two babies. I think they'll both make it."

"I hope so. How long before they can fly?"

"If all goes well, less than two months. They'll be on their own by fall."

"Then your job will be over?"

"It will, but this is only a stopgap until I get another full-time state job, or maybe something with the national parks."

"It's a pretty cool temp job, though. It would be exciting to see those little ones fly for the first time."

"I hope to. If I don't personally catch it with my still camera, I'm hoping the webcam will. Is the father still there?"

"Yep." Luke shifted his weight and the platform creaked. "But I think he's about done with the feeding routine. There he goes. Now the babies are huddling down."

"Unless the mother comes back, there won't be much to see for a while."

"No sign of her." Luke lowered the binoculars and crouched down next to the webcam. "So this is on 24/7?"

"Yes. Fortunately it has a zoom, so the pictures are pretty good, but quite a few researchers prefer to mount the camera on the tree where the nest is."

He glanced over his shoulder at her. "How the hell would you do something like that without freaking out the eagles?"

"You have to mount it before they start nesting and then hope they come back to that same place." She powered down the laptop to save her battery. "The professor who hired me hopes to get someone to monitor the nest next year and see if the pair returns. This year, by the time someone discovered the nest, the eggs were already laid, which meant this was the best we could do."

He stood and turned back to her. "Are you hooked up to the internet so you can broadcast it? I've seen people do that."

"So have I, but that wouldn't work here because of the location."

He glanced around. “Too remote?”

“No, too accessible. The professor doesn’t want the place overrun by tourists trying to see the eagles up close and personal, which could disturb them. The Chance family isn’t too eager to have that happen, either. Eventually, with proper supervision, the Chances might approve an ecotour back here, but it would be carefully planned.”

“Makes sense. So this is a strictly private study.”

“It is. The professor would be up here himself if he could manage it. He’s the only one who gets the webcam feed, and I send him written reports.”

“Am I breaking any rules by being up here?”

She smiled. “It’s not *that* hush-hush. Everybody on the ranch knows about the eagles, and quite a few people in town. Fortunately, we’re a protective bunch of folks around here, so the eagles should be safe.”

“I think you’re right about that. I’ve only lived here since the end of October, but I can tell it’s a close community. You take care of your own.”

So she was right—he was a fairly recent hire at the ranch. Getting one piece of the puzzle made her curious to find out more. “What brought you here?”

“More a *who* than a *what.* Nash Bledsoe. He was my boss when he co-owned a riding stable in Sacramento with Lindsay, his former wife. She wasn’t much fun to work for after he left. Actually, she wasn’t much fun to work for while he was there. I stayed because of him. Once he moved back here, I asked him to put in a good word at the Last Chance, and here I am.”

"And now Nash has his own place, the Triple G. Are you headed there next?"

He shook his head. "Wouldn't be fair to Nash. I tend to move on after about a year, no matter where I am, so my time's two-thirds gone. He needs a ranch hand who'll stick around longer than a few months."

"You leave after a year?" She'd never heard anything so ridiculous in her life, unless he was trying to escape a woman or the law. "Are you on the run?"

"Nope." He smiled.

She looked into those smiling brown eyes. He didn't seem to be hiding anything. "Then I don't get it."

"Most people don't. It's just the way I like it. New scenery, new people. Keeps things interesting."

She should have known there'd be a fly in the ointment. He might be the sexiest man she'd met in ages, but if he avoided all attachments, then she literally couldn't see any future in getting to know him.

"That bothers you, doesn't it?" He sounded disappointed.

She shrugged. "Not really." At least it shouldn't. She'd leaped to some unwarranted conclusions about how this would go, and now he'd set her straight. At least he'd told her up front, so she could back off. "It's your life. You're entitled to live it the way you want to."

"Yes, I am." He sighed. "But I guess I'll pay the price where you're concerned."

"What price?"

"I...was hoping to get to know you better."

"Oh?" She wondered if this was leading where she thought it was. "In what way?"

"Well, I thought we might become friends."

"Sure, Luke. We can become friends." But from the way he'd flirted with her earlier, she didn't think he was looking for a platonic relationship. Maybe she was wrong. "You can come out here and check on the eagles from time to time, and we'll chat. Is that what you had in mind?"

"Uh…no." He rubbed the back of his neck and looked off in the distance, clearly uncomfortable with the discussion. "See, the thing is, I thought, from the way you looked at me back there at the stream, that you might be willing to go a little beyond friendship."

How embarrassing that he'd read her so accurately. "I see."

"But I can tell you don't like the idea that I don't stay around. Your attitude toward me changed."

"You act as if that's hard to understand. Do most of the women you meet like the idea of a temporary affair?"

"They do, actually." His gaze was earnest. "I tend to be attracted to women who have something going on in their lives, like you. The last thing they want is some needy guy who wants to monopolize them. So we get together, have great discussions, great sex and no strings attached."

"That must suit your lifestyle perfectly." Having this discussion while he stood there looking virile as hell wasn't helping. She didn't want to want him. He was a girl-in-every-port sort of guy. And yet…her insides quivered at the tantalizing possibilities.

"It does suit me, and it seems to suit them. I jumped

to conclusions about you, though. I thought you'd be happy to hear my exit plan, but you're not."

She cleared her throat to give herself some time to think. He was right about the signals she'd been giving off, so she couldn't blame him for putting her in the same category as his other girlfriends. Maybe she *was* in that category and hadn't realized it.

Although she'd like to settle down someday, she hadn't yet felt compelled to do that. She'd been building her career in wildlife research in Florida, but that had petered out. She hoped to get another full-time job in her field, which could be anywhere in the country. She didn't want to be either saved or tied down by a guy.

But in the meantime, she was going through a period of sexual deprivation, and he'd suggested a reprieve from that. Was it so terrible that he wasn't into making a lifelong commitment, especially when she wasn't looking for that, either?

"I need some time to think about this," she said. "After all, I just met you."

"Fair enough." He moved closer. "Just to be clear, are you saving yourself for Mr. Right? Because I'm not that guy."

She struggled to breathe normally, but she kept drawing in the intoxicating scent of Luke Griffin. "I'm not saving myself for anyone, but I…" She lost track of what she'd meant to say. This was her brain on lust, and it was fried.

"Then think about it." His lips hovered closer. "And while you're thinking, consider this." His mouth came down on hers.

She should pull away. She should give herself more time to review the situation with cold, hard logic before she allowed him to influence her by… Oh, no… he was good at this…very good. Before she realized it, he'd invaded her mouth with his tongue. No, that wasn't true. She'd invited him in. There had been no invasion at all, because she wanted…everything.

He lifted his head.

She didn't want the kiss to be over, but she wasn't going to beg him to do it again. A girl had to have some pride, which was why she wasn't about to open her eyes and let him see the turmoil he'd created.

His breath was warm on her lips. "Think about it. I'll come back for your answer." There was a movement of air and the sound of him climbing back down the ladder.

Opening her eyes, she sat down on the platform and held her hand against her pounding heart. She'd never deliberately set out to have a no-strings affair. But he'd been so sweet about it.

Still, she wasn't the type of woman he thought she was. Her answer should be no. Shouldn't it?

3

LUKE THOUGHT ABOUT Naomi all the way back to the Last Chance Ranch. He was worried that he'd insulted her by the way he'd acted. The thing was, her behavior toward him had been *exactly* like the women he'd known in the past.

In those cases, instant chemistry had been followed by a clear understanding. Sex would be purely for fun, because the intelligent ladies he'd connected with had other things to do besides take care of a man and his ego. They'd considered him a gift because he required nothing of them but multiple orgasms.

If Naomi didn't fit that category, he'd definitely insulted her, which didn't sit well with him. He knew the guy to talk to—Emmett Sterling. Emmett had helped her set up out there and might give him some insight into her character.

But he'd have to be careful. He didn't want any of the other cowhands hearing such a conversation. Luke hoped he could find a quiet moment to speak man-to-man with Emmett, but when he arrived back at the ranch he wondered if that would be possible.

Emmett, along with Sarah Chance's fiancé, Pete Beckett, had eight adolescent boys in the main corral for a roping clinic. The boys were all part of Pete's program to help disadvantaged youth. By living and working alongside cowboys several weeks out of the summer, they had an opportunity to learn discipline and routine.

Luke didn't see much of either going on in the corral. Ropes flew helter-skelter. They caught indiscriminately on fence posts and people. Clearly at least one more adult was needed in that arena.

The boys had been in residence for a couple of weeks, so Luke already knew them all pretty well. Wading into the confusion was no problem for him. He called out a greeting to Emmett and Pete, who seemed overjoyed to see him.

"I'll take these two." He motioned to Ace, a skinny, dark-haired, tattooed boy with attitude sticking out all over him, and his unlikely friend, a pudgy blond boy named Eddie who was always eager to please. Nash had been their favorite cowboy on the ranch, but Nash was busy with his own neighboring ranch these days, so Luke had stepped in. By pulling Ace out of the confusion, Luke knew he'd remove fifty percent of the problem. Ace resisted being told what to do, but he had no trouble telling everyone else what they should be doing.

Luke brought them next to the fence. "Roping is not only a skill," he said, "but an art." He'd figured out that beneath the tough exterior, Ace had the soul of a poet.

"Not when I do it," Ace grumbled.

"That's because you're treating it like a sport."

Eddie slapped his coiled rope against his thigh. "It *is* a sport." He peered at Luke. "Isn't it?"

"It can be both, I guess, but when it's done with style, it's more than a sport. It's an art form. Can I borrow your rope, Eddie?"

Eddie handed over his rope.

"Anybody can throw a loop and catch something," Luke said.

"Not me," Ace muttered.

"The trick is to make that loop dance." Luke had always loved the supple feel of a good rope. He'd been lucky enough to learn the skill from an expert roper on a ranch in eastern Washington. Luke roped the way he made love, with concentration, subtlety and—he hoped—finesse.

But he didn't like to show off, so he'd never demonstrated his skills to the folks at the Last Chance. Nash had known, but Nash would never have embarrassed him by making him perform on command like some trained monkey.

Ace needed a demonstration, though, because the kid wouldn't be interested unless he could see the beauty inherent in the task. Luke built his loop and proceeded to show him. Not only did he make the loop dance, but *he* danced, leaping and weaving in and out of the undulating circle he'd created.

He was so involved that he didn't realize all other activity had ceased and he'd drawn a rapt audience. He figured it out when he allowed the rope to settle at his feet and people started clapping. Glancing around, he saw that he'd brought the clinic to a halt.

"Hey, I'm sorry," he said. "I didn't mean to interrupt the proceedings."

"I'm glad you did." Pete surveyed the circle of admiring boys. "You've just become our new roping instructor. Welcome to the staff."

"Why didn't you tell us you could twirl a rope like that, son?" Emmett asked. "I had no idea."

"It never came up."

"He didn't tell you because he's too cool to brag." Ace's hero worship echoed in every syllable. Then he gazed up at Luke, his expression intense. "I want to learn how to do that."

"Good. I can teach you."

"Teach me, too!" Eddie's comment was followed by a chorus of others.

"Looks like you have a group of eager students," Pete said. "We'll be your assistants."

The rest of the afternoon passed quickly as Luke worked with the boys. He didn't remember he'd skipped lunch until his stomach started to growl.

As the boys were herded off to have dinner at the main house, Emmett came over and hooked an arm around Luke's shoulder. "I'm buying you a hamburger and a beer at the Spirits and Spurs. You rode in like the cavalry today, and I appreciate it."

"Thank you. I accept." Luke recognized a golden opportunity when it was presented, and he wasn't about to turn down the chance to talk to Emmett about Naomi. "Give me twenty minutes to shower and change."

"You got it. I need to freshen up a bit, myself. I'll bring my truck around to the side of the bunkhouse."

Within half an hour Luke was sitting in the passenger seat of Emmett's old but well-maintained pickup as they traveled the ten miles from the ranch to the little town of Shoshone and the popular bar. They rode with the windows down, and every once in a while they'd pass a stretch of road where the crickets were chirping like crazy.

It was one of those nights that wasn't too hot and wasn't too cold—the perfect night for lovers. Luke thought of Naomi, who was probably tucked into her tent right now. Before he'd ridden away, he'd made a quick survey and located that tent, a faded blue dome-style.

She was probably fine. Yet whenever he thought of her by herself, he had the urge to head on out there and make sure she was okay. That might not be particularly evolved, and an independent woman like Naomi wouldn't appreciate an overprotective attitude from anyone, let alone some cowboy she'd just met. Funny, he didn't usually have those protective feelings toward women, but with Naomi he couldn't seem to help himself.

Right now, though, he had to stop worrying about Naomi sleeping alone in her tent and grab this chance for a private discussion with Emmett. He didn't want to blow it. Once they arrived at their destination, their privacy would disappear.

Luke took a steadying breath. "I mentioned that

I was riding out to check on Naomi Perkins today, right?"

"I believe you said something like that. Did you go?"

"I did, and she's surviving great out there. It's pretty amazing to look at those baby eagles."

"So you climbed up to the platform?"

"She was nice enough to ask me, so I did. You built one hell of an observation spot for her, Emmett. She's really set up well."

"Good. I'm glad it's working out for her. I kept meaning to go out and I haven't made it, so I'm glad you did. She's a scrappy little thing, but I can't help worrying about her sometimes. Her mom and dad worry, too, but they've told me they've worked hard to give her room to be herself."

All that fit with what Luke had sensed about her from the beginning. "So I guess she's a modern woman who doesn't need a man around to protect her."

Emmett didn't answer right away. "If you mean that she doesn't need a man to physically protect her, that's probably right," he said at last. "She took karate when she was still in high school, and she could flip me onto my back if she wanted to."

Luke thought about that. "Good to know."

"And she takes other precautions. She has bear spray, and she makes sure her food is stowed. Naomi has a better chance of surviving out there by herself than some men I've known. But…"

"But?" Luke waited for the other shoe to drop.

"I could be way off base, but I don't think she's a

true loner. I think she'd love to find somebody to share her life, as long as it was the right somebody."

"Hmm." Well, that sealed his fate. He couldn't mess around with a woman like that. If Naomi yearned for someone steady in her life, he'd back off. His free-spirited father had tied himself to a job, a wife and a mortgage. He obviously regretted his choices. Luke had inherited that same free spirit, and he had no intention of repeating his dad's mistakes.

"Then again, how should I know what's in Naomi's heart?" Emmett said. "I'm the last person who should give out opinions on such things. I'm a divorced man in love with a wonderful woman, but the idea of marrying her scares me shitless."

"That's not so hard to understand, Emmett. Pam Mulholland has big bucks and you're a man of modest means. I watched my buddy Nash fall into the trap of marrying a woman who had a pile of money, and it was a disaster." Luke paused. "Then again, he's now planning to marry Bethany Grace, who also has a pile of money, and I think it'll be fine."

Emmett sighed. "So it all depends on the woman. And I know in my heart that Pam wouldn't let the money be a problem, but my damned pride is at stake. I can't seem to overcome my basic reluctance to marry a wealthy woman when I'm certainly not wealthy myself. I'm afraid I'll feel like a gigolo."

Luke dipped his head to hide a smile. The interior of the truck was dim. Still, he didn't want to take the slightest chance that Emmett would see that smile. But if Emmett Sterling, the quintessential rugged cowboy, could label himself a gigolo, the world had turned completely upside down.

NAOMI HAD MEANT to spend one more night out at the research site before hiking back to Shoshone for supplies and clean clothes. But the visit from Luke had thrown her off balance. She decided to take her break that very afternoon.

After clearing her platform of everything except the webcam and securing her campsite, she hoisted her backpack and made the trek into town. A night sleeping in her childhood bed at her parents' house would be a welcome luxury.

Her folks were thrilled to see her, as always, but business was brisk at the Shoshone Diner and they didn't have much time to chat. She'd anticipated that. At one time the diner served only breakfast and lunch, but recently they'd added a dinner menu.

Prior to that, the Spirits and Spurs had been the only place in town that served an evening meal. But as the tourist business had grown and the wait time for a table at the Spirits and Spurs had become ridiculous, Naomi's parents had decided to expand their offerings.

It had paid off for them. They'd hired extra help because Naomi wasn't there to waitress anymore, and both women were capable and had a set routine. If Naomi hung around the diner tonight, she'd only get in everybody's way.

So she ate the meat loaf her mother insisted on feeding her, went home for a quick shower and a change of clothes, and walked over to the Spirits and Spurs. On the way, she thought of Luke, who quite likely wouldn't be there on a weeknight. Ranch hands generally came into town on the weekend.

As she walked toward the intersection where the bar was located, she remembered the foolishly grand entrance she'd envisioned making in her tight jeans and revealing blouse. Instead she'd pulled on her comfort outfit—faded jeans and a soft knit top in her favorite shade of red. Nothing about her appearance tonight was calculated to turn heads.

Ah, well. She'd scrapped her plan to knock Luke back on his heels and make him her slave. Luke didn't intend to be any woman's slave. He was a love-'em-and-leave-'em kind of cowboy.

She'd never met a man who'd laid it out so clearly. At first she'd been appalled by the concept of a relationship based mostly on sex, with some interesting conversations thrown in, a relationship with an expiration date stamped plainly on the package.

She laughed to herself. And what a package it was, too. That was part of her dilemma. She wanted that package, even if she could enjoy it for only a limited time.

Music from the Spirits and Spurs beckoned her as she approached. During tourist season the bar had a live band every night, and Naomi loved to dance. She wouldn't mind kicking up her heels a little if anyone inside the bar felt like getting out on the floor. She could do with a little fun.

Maybe that was how she should view Luke's suggestion, too. She'd never seen herself as the kind of woman who would have a casual fling, but maybe she was needlessly limiting herself. She might be back in her hometown, but she wasn't a kid anymore. She had the right to make adult decisions. Very adult. A sensual zing heated her blood.

If the thought of parading her behavior in front of her parents bothered her at all, and she admitted that it did, they wouldn't have to know. She was living out in the woods, away from prying eyes. Luke might have to explain his behavior if he made regular visits to her campsite, but she'd let him worry about that.

As she pushed open the door to the Spirits and Spurs, the familiar scent of beer and smoke greeted her. This bar might end up being the last place in the entire world to ban smoking. Even if they did, the place was supposed to be haunted by the ghosts of cowboys and prospectors who'd tipped a few in this building a century ago. No doubt they'd bring the aroma of tobacco with them.

The band started playing a recent Alan Jackson hit she happened to like. Couples filled the small dance floor. The place was jumping, with most of the round wooden tables occupied and very few vacant seats at the bar.

Coming here had been a good idea. She watched the dancers and tapped her foot in time to the music. She'd have a beer and dance if she found a willing partner. Then tomorrow, or whenever Luke came back for his answer, she'd tell him not only yes but hell, yes. Look out, world. Naomi Perkins was ready to cut loose.

"Naomi?"

The rich baritone made her whirl in its direction. She'd last heard that voice after being kissed senseless twenty feet above the ground. She found herself staring into Luke Griffin's brown-eyed gaze. Her heart launched into overdrive.

They spoke in unison. "What are you doing here?"

"You first." Luke tilted back his hat and stared at her. "You're the big surprise. I thought you'd be curled up in your blue dome tent fast asleep."

She fought the urge to grab his shirtfront in both hands and pull him into another kiss, one even more potent than what they'd shared earlier today. "I'm staying with my folks in town. And how do you know I have a blue dome tent?"

"I checked it out before I left."

"For future reference?"

"No. In fact, that's why I hotfooted it over here. I—" He gestured toward the band. "Love that song, but I don't want to have to yell over it. Can we move outside for a minute?"

"Okay." She gulped in air and did her best to calm down. When she agreed to this affair, she wanted to appear in command of herself, even if she wasn't. He was used to sophistication, and she would exude that.

He held the door open and she walked out into the soft night air. He followed. As the door closed behind him, the music faded into background noise.

She turned to him. "Luke, I'm glad you're here tonight, because—"

"No, wait. Let me say something first. I was off base today, and I apologize with all my heart. You're not that kind of woman. I made a mistake and no doubt insulted you in the process."

Yikes, now what? Right when she'd decided to accept his outrageous proposal, he'd withdrawn it on the grounds that she wasn't *that kind of woman.*

She swallowed. "What kind of woman do you think I am?"

"The kind who needs stability. You deserve someone who wants to become a permanent part of your life, and I'm not that guy."

"Luke, I don't know what my life is going to be yet. You made me do some serious thinking today. I was shocked by your assumption that I'd want a fling, but—"

"I know you were, and I feel pretty rotten about that."

"Yes, but you see, when it comes right down to it..." She placed both hands on his chest so she could feel his heart beating and know for sure that it was racing as fast as hers. This wasn't a cold, calculated decision, after all. It was being made in the heat of the moment, and she was ready to dive headfirst into the flames.

She looked into his beautiful eyes. "I do want a fling with you, Luke." Heat sizzled through her as she plunged into the fire. "In fact, I can't think of anything I want more."

4

LUKE WAS SUDDENLY so short of breath that he was a little scared he might black out. That wouldn't be cool in front of this woman who'd said she wanted to have sex with him. But he couldn't kiss her until he stopped struggling to fill his lungs with air.

The corners of her beautiful mouth tipped up. "Apparently you didn't expect me to say that."

"No." He dragged in a breath. "That's a fact. I definitely did not."

"I've never had this kind of effect on a man before." She gazed up at him as amusement turned to concern. "Are you going to be all right?"

"I'm going to be terrific." There. That statement sounded normal. Finally trusting himself to wrap her in his arms, he nudged his hat back with his thumb and pulled her close. Damn, that felt good. "*We're* going to be terrific."

"I'll have to leave that up to you." Her eyes caught the sparkle from the bar's neon bucking bronco. "If you've spent your adult life playing the field, then I guarantee you have more experience than I do."

"Maybe." He aligned his body with hers. They fit so perfectly it was a little scary for a guy who didn't believe in perfect fits. But he'd figured that she'd be soft and pliable, warm and willing. His cock responded quickly. He'd have to remember they were standing on the corner of the town's only intersection. "But I can recognize natural talent when I see it."

Her smile widened. "You think I have a natural talent for sex?"

"I know you do, at least for kissing, which usually tells me a lot about a woman." Keeping one arm firmly around her narrow waist, he slid his free hand up through her silky blond hair. No ponytail tonight.

"We only kissed once."

"True." He cradled the back of her head. "I should gather more information before I come to any firm conclusions."

She rocked against him. "Feels like you've already come to a very firm conclusion."

"See, that's what I'm talking about." Cupping her bottom, he snuggled her in tight. "A natural talent. And, lady, sassy comments and sexy moves like that will get you anything you want from me."

"Anything?"

"Sky's the limit." He lowered his head and brushed his mouth over hers. So delicious. But he dared not get involved in the kind of kiss he wanted, the kind that would make him forget where he was.

She clutched his shoulders and joined in his little

game of butterfly kisses. "I've already told you what I want."

"In general terms, yes." The feathery touch of her lips could drive him crazy if it went on too long without some way to release the tension. "But we have to work out the details."

"We can't do anything here."

He chuckled. "No, obviously not." Although with the blood pumping hot in his veins, he'd already fantasized about coaxing her into the shadows behind the building. "We're standing in front of the most popular spot in town."

"I mean not here, as in not in Shoshone."

He nibbled her full lower lip. "You want to drive to Jackson?" He hoped not. He wouldn't be able to swing very many trips to Jackson and still handle his assigned work on the ranch. But with a hot woman in his arms, he was ready to do whatever it took to have her.

"No, nothing that drastic." She placed tiny kisses at the corners of his mouth. "I was referring to my campsite as being the most discreet choice."

"It's perfect, except you're not there." And he wanted her now, tonight. Moments ago he'd given up all hope of a relationship, but her unexpected decision and these flirty kisses had flipped the switch on his libido and destroyed his patience. He outlined her mouth with the tip of his tongue.

Her breathing had changed, signaling that she was getting as worked up as he was. "I will be there."

"When?" His fingers flexed against her bottom.

"Tomorrow."

He groaned. "That's forever."

"I can't hike out there in the dark."

"I know. But I—whoops, somebody's coming." He released her and stepped back. With luck, whoever it was would simply call a greeting and pass on by. Then he glanced over and realized that wasn't going to happen. Thank God for the shadows that should keep his aroused condition from being too obvious.

Emmett walked toward them. "Hi there, Naomi." He touched the brim of his hat. "Nice to see you."

"Hi, Emmett. It's good to see you, too. You don't usually come into town midweek."

"I wanted to treat Luke. He showed up in the nick of time and put on a roping demonstration that saved what was fast becoming a disaster."

"Ah, you would have worked it out." Luke pulled the brim of his hat back down and hoped Emmett hadn't noticed how he'd shoved it back, which was typical for a cowboy who'd been kissing a woman.

"I'm not so sure." Emmett glanced at Naomi. "Take my word for it. We had a snarled-up mess, but five minutes after Luke showed up and started twirling a rope, the kids were mesmerized. They hadn't seen the possibilities of roping until then. Pete and I aren't that fancy. This boy has hidden talents."

"Talent, singular," Luke said. "Trick roping. That's my only hidden talent."

Naomi glanced at him. "Oh, I doubt that."

"Anyway," Emmett said. "I didn't mean to break up your conversation, Luke, but your food's getting cold.

Naomi, why don't you join us? We have an extra chair. Have you had dinner?"

"Yes, thanks. I ate at the diner before I came over. But I don't want to keep you two from your meal. Let's go in."

"Excellent. You can fill me in on how the eagle project's going."

"I'd love to. That platform you and Jack built is working out beautifully."

Luke followed them in. As Emmett asked more questions about the eagles, Luke quietly ground a centimeter off his back molars. He hadn't been sure when Emmett first showed up, but he was now. The foreman was deliberately interfering in what he saw as a problem situation between Luke and Naomi.

No doubt Emmett saw Luke as the aggressor and Naomi as the sweet local girl about to be seduced by a guy who would leave her in the lurch. It wasn't like that, of course. Luke had been ready to back off and Naomi had turned the tables on him. But he couldn't very well explain that to Emmett. A gentleman wouldn't put the blame on a lady.

The foreman had every reason to misunderstand what was happening. When Luke had been hired on at the Last Chance, he'd warned both Emmett and Jack that he tended to move along after a year or so. They'd both predicted he'd change his mind, that the Last Chance had a way of getting in a person's blood.

But last month he'd turned down Nash's offer of employment and had made no secret as to why. He believed in being up front with people, so he could see why Emmett thought Naomi needed someone to step in and keep her heart from being broken.

Luke didn't want to get crossways with the foreman. He liked and admired the guy, and until now they'd had no real issues between them. But Luke would be damned if he'd allow Emmett to louse up a perfectly acceptable arrangement between two consenting adults.

He thought about his options as he ate the excellent dinner Emmett had bought him and listened to the foreman and Naomi talk about the eagles. Luke even participated in the conversation because he was interested in those birds, too. He was more interested in the woman watching the birds, but he found the eagle study fascinating. He hadn't been kidding when he'd told Naomi that an eagle's freedom of movement appealed to him.

"That nest's not as big as some." Naomi took a sip of the draft she'd ordered. "It's only about seven feet across. I've seen reports on nests that are ten feet and weigh close to two tons."

Emmett shook his head in disbelief. "That's like putting my pickup in the top branches of one of those pines. I had no idea they could be that heavy. I'd—" He stopped talking and glanced at the door. "What do you know? There's Pam. Excuse me a minute, folks. I need to go over and say hello. Maybe she can join us." He stood and walked toward the door.

Luke grabbed his chance. He kept his voice low as he looked over at Naomi. "You do realize Emmett's trying to save you from me, right?"

"I thought he might be."

"He told me earlier tonight that he thought you wanted a steady guy in your life. That's why I backed off."

Naomi sighed. "I'm not surprised he'd say something like that. He's friends with my parents, and he's a dad. He probably sees me as being like his daughter, Emily."

"Ah. Okay, I get that." Luke thought about the blonde woman who was in training to eventually take over Emmett's job when he retired. Emily and Naomi had several things in common besides their coloring. They were both only children who had been raised to be independent and fend for themselves without leaning on a man. They both enjoyed testing themselves with physical challenges.

But Emily was now married to Clay Whitaker, who ran the stud operation for the Last Chance. Emmett might figure that Naomi, having similarities to his daughter, also should find herself someone like Clay.

He glanced at her. "Maybe Emmett knows what he's talking about. Maybe I should just—"

"Don't you dare back off because Emmett thinks I'm just like his daughter. I'm not."

The defiant sparks flashing in her blue eyes gladdened his heart. She thought for herself, and that was a quality he admired. "I'm sure you're not just like anyone."

"Nobody is. We're all unique, which means we get to choose our own path. What you and I decide to do is none of Emmett's business."

The tension that had been tightening a spot between Luke's shoulder blades eased. "And you won't be upset if I tell him that?"

"No, but I think I'm the one who needs to tell him."

"I'll tell him." He started to add that it should be a man-to-man talk but decided that might not sit well with Naomi. She liked being in charge of her destiny.

"No, you work for him and I don't."

"But he built you a research platform."

"Well, one of us needs to say something. Uh-oh. Here he comes. And he doesn't look happy."

"Bet it has something to do with Pam." Luke noticed that Pam Mulholland, the woman Emmett cared for but couldn't bring himself to marry, was being helped into her chair by a guy Luke didn't recognize. The barrel-chested man dressed in flashy Western clothes and what looked like an expensive hat. "Or that guy."

Emmett returned to his seat, his expression grim. "It's my own damned fault," he muttered to no one in particular.

"What is?" Luke asked. "And who is that guy with Pam? I've never seen him before, and if that's the way he normally dresses, I doubt I've missed him."

"You haven't missed him." Emmett picked up his beer and drained the contents. "Name's Clifford Mason. Just flew in today from Denver. Booked a room at the Bunk and Grub."

Naomi looked over at the table where Pam and the newcomer sat. "Does Pam normally go out to dinner with her B and B guests?"

"No, she does not." Emmett smoothed his mustache. "Far as I know, it's never happened before."

Luke could see Emmett was seething with jealousy and was doing his best to keep a lid on his feelings. "Is he on vacation?"

"No, he's been in contact with both Pam and Tyler Keller, Josie's sister-in-law." Emmett looked over at Naomi. "I don't know if your folks told you that the town hired Tyler a while back as a special-events planner to bring in more business. She's been doing a great job."

"I think Mom and Dad said something about it. And I certainly see the results in the increased tourist trade. So this guy is connected to an event?"

Emmett nodded. "Something to do with special preparations for the Fourth of July celebration. All very hush-hush. They want to surprise the good people of Shoshone."

"Well, then." Luke sat back in his chair. "It's only a business dinner. He'll be around until everything's set up, and then he'll leave. No big deal, right?"

Emmett scowled at him. "It wouldn't be if I hadn't seen the way he looked at Pam, like she was a helping of his favorite dessert."

"That's understandable." Naomi seemed to be trying to soothe the troubled waters, too. "She's a beautiful woman. But there's no way she'd prefer a citified dandy like him to you, Emmett. She probably went to dinner with him to be polite."

"I'd be willing to believe that if she hadn't flirted with him right under my damned nose."

Naomi smiled. “Emmett, that’s the oldest trick in the book. She’s trying to make you jealous. Everybody knows how you feel about her. And she’s made no secret about how she feels about you, too. Why not end the suspense and propose to her?”

“Can’t bring myself to do it. Doesn’t seem right when she has so much and I have so little.”

“Love?” Naomi asked with a twinkle in her eye.

Emmett snorted. “’Course not. Money’s the problem, not love.”

Luke checked on Pam and Clifford’s table. “Then you’re leaving the door open for the likes of him. I agree with Naomi. I’m sure Pam would rather have you than that character. But she might be tired of waiting for you to get over this hang-up.”

Emmett muttered something that could have been a curse.

“I have an idea.” Luke tucked his napkin beside his plate. “Go over and ask Pam to dance. Stake your claim.”

The light of battle lit Emmett’s blue eyes as he pushed back his chair. “All right, I will. That sonofabitch probably can’t dance a lick.”

Luke grinned. “If he could, he wouldn’t dress like a peacock.”

“That was brilliant,” Naomi murmured as they watched Emmett amble over to the table.

“Let’s hope it works.” Luke thought it might. He hadn’t spent his adult life romancing women without learning a thing or two. Pam looked surprised, but she left her chair and walked to the dance floor with Emmett.

Luke pushed back his chair. “That’s our cue. Dance with me, Naomi Perkins.”

Laughing, she took the hand he offered and soon he had her right where he wanted her, in his arms. He’d had a hunch that she’d be a good dancer. He thanked the series of coincidences that had given him the opportunity to dance with Naomi. What a joy.

Her breath was warm in his ear as she twirled with him on the polished floor. “Did you talk Emmett into dancing for his sake or yours?”

“I figured it would help us both out.” He spun her around. “I couldn’t leave here tonight without at least one dance.”

She brushed a quick kiss on his cheek. “I knew you had more hidden talents.”

“Anything I have is yours for the taking.” He moved her smoothly across the floor in a spirited two-step.

“I’m taking it.”

“When?”

“I’ll be up on my platform by ten in the morning. After that, it’s up to you.”

He twirled her under his arm. “Are you sure we can’t manage something tonight?”

“Positive. You’re going home with Emmett and I’m sleeping in my parents’ house.”

He brought her in close for one precious second. His heart hammered so loudly he could barely hear the music. “I want you so much.”

"I want you, too." Her cheeks were flushed. "And I will have you. And you'll have me. Tomorrow."

The music ended, and he held her close. "Promise you'll think about me when you're lying alone tonight."

She gazed up at him, her lips parted as she breathed quickly, recovering from the exertion of the dance. "Only if you'll promise to think about me."

"That's an easy promise."

"I think I should leave now." She eased out of his arms. "See you tomorrow."

He watched her go and fought the urge to follow her outside for one last kiss.

"That was a good idea you had." Emmett came over and clapped him on the shoulder. "We dance great together, and I don't think she'll be flirting with that Clifford guy so much now. Thanks, son."

"You're welcome. Ready to go home?"

"Yeah. I made my statement." He reached for his wallet and tossed some bills on the table. "Let's leave."

Back in Emmett's truck, they rode in silence for a couple of miles. But finally Luke decided he needed to clear the air. "I know you're worried about me getting involved with Naomi."

Emmett blew out a breath. "I wouldn't be, except you keep talking about leaving. I wish you'd rethink that, Luke. Frankly, I've never quite understood it."

"I have more things to see and do. Too long in one place and I get restless, wondering what's on the other side of the hill. When you start getting attached is when you're reluctant to leave, and then you slowly settle into your rut."

"I suppose you think I'm in a rut, then."

"From my vantage point, yes, but if you're happy, that's all that matters. I was born a wanderer, just like my dad."

Emmett slowed down so that a family of raccoons could cross the road. "So he travels all over the place, too?"

"Nope. He got mired in a mortgage, car payments, a lawn that has to be mowed, a fence that has to be painted, a garage that has to be cleaned. My mother wanted all that, and he became trapped by those things in order to please her, or at least keep the peace. He never went anywhere. He warned me that he was a cautionary tale."

"Hmm. So your father is miserable?"

Luke nodded. "Not completely miserable, but he has regrets. He sighs when he glances through the travel section of the newspaper and he watches every travel documentary he can find. He even clips out coupons for discount travel adventures that he can't follow up on."

"Excuse me for saying so, Luke, but unless he's an invalid, he could still travel. What's stopping him from going?"

"Like I said, the responsibilities at home, and my mother, who has no interest in traveling." But as Luke laid it out for Emmett, he had to admit that his father was an adult with free will. If this was his passion, he could find a way to make it happen. Maybe it was easier to stay home and complain.

"You know, son, could be he's using your mother as an excuse not to go."

"Maybe. He might be scared to actually go now. I see your point, but that only emphasizes mine. I don't want to tie myself to the same things that weigh him down, whether he's allowing that or not. I'd rather avoid being in that mess in the first place. I wouldn't be good at settling down, and I know it."

"I suppose, with an example like that, you don't think so."

Luke had the feeling that Emmett had more he could say, but he was refraining from saying it. That was okay with Luke, because they'd strayed from the topic, which was his intentions toward Naomi and hers toward him.

So he tackled the subject again. "Naomi knows all about my wanderlust. She and I are attracted to each other, and I've told her I'm not a forever kind of guy."

"Yes, but she might think she can change you."

"I don't think she wants to."

"All women want to get a man to settle down. It's the way of the world." Emmett spoke with certainty.

"It used to be, Emmett, but not so much anymore. Naomi's like a lot of women—not sure where she's going, what her next job will be. She wants to stay flexible. She's no more ready for a husband than I'm ready for a wife."

"She told you that?"

"She did. And she's not the only woman who's said the same kind of thing. I don't want to go behind your back, Emmett, but I intend to spend time with Naomi, and she's heading into it with her eyes wide open. In fact, she likes the idea that I won't be begging for her hand in marriage."

Emmett was quiet for at least a full minute. "Her folks wouldn't appreciate knowing about this."

"I'm sure they wouldn't."

"So I won't tell them."

"Thank you."

"I won't pry into your activities during your free time, but I expect the same amount of work out of you that I've always had."

"You'll get it. But I have an afternoon off coming, and I'd like to take it tomorrow."

"Guess I don't have to ask where you'll be going."

"No. And…I'd like to borrow a horse. If you can't lend me one, I understand, but I—"

"You can borrow the damned horse." Emmett sounded gruff. "Smudge can always use the exercise."

"Thanks, Emmett."

"You're welcome. And if you have any more bright ideas regarding Pam, don't keep them to yourself."

Luke smiled. "I won't."

5

Naomi had expected to toss and turn, but she slept great. She loved camping, but there was something to be said for a good innerspring. As she packed up for the hike back to the campsite, she thought about what likely would be happening there in the next few days and searched around for items she wouldn't normally take camping.

Lacy underwear topped the list. Then she threw in a see-through nightgown that she'd never considered wearing while sleeping in a tent. She had a perfume bottle in her hand, ready to pack it, when she came to her senses.

Good grief, had she completely lost her mind? Fragrance of any kind was a no-no. She was in bear country, for God's sake, not at a beach resort.

For that matter, she might want to forget the see-through nightgown, too. It was the sort of thing a woman wore when she emerged from the bathroom of a luxury suite and sashayed over to the king-size bed where her lover waited, his gaze hot. When two people were crammed into a small dome tent, transparent lingerie lost most of its impact.

With reality smacking her in the face, she pulled out her lacy underwear, too. She was doing field research on a nesting pair of eagles, not arranging a romantic tryst with the man of her dreams. Luke had suggested this arrangement after catching her at her rumpled worst. If she got all fancy on him, he might laugh.

Or worse yet, he might wonder if she was trying to snare him with her feminine wiles. Then he'd turn tail and run. He'd proposed a straightforward liaison where they both understood the parameters. Seductive clothing could easily send the wrong message.

Because she could cut cross-country to the campsite, her hike was only about five miles. Hiking always helped her think. As she walked, she examined her knee-jerk response to this situation with Luke.

She'd automatically reached for the accepted female lures—fragrance and suggestive clothing. She'd reacted as if she needed to make herself more desirable to him. Oh, yeah, Luke would have been suspicious of her motivation for doing that.

She was suspicious of her motivation. Before this affair started, she might want to search her conscience to make absolutely sure no hidden agenda existed. This relationship couldn't be a bait and switch where she accepted his invitation to a no-strings affair and then subtly tried to bind him to her.

Hiking across a sunny meadow filled with sage and wildflowers, butterflies and songbirds, was perfect for soul-searching. She did a mental practice run through the scenario. For a few weeks, she would enjoy Luke's company and his gorgeous body. They'd have great sex and watch the eagles together. She'd become used to having him around.

But the eagles would leave the nest. Luke had already said that was about the time he planned to head for parts unknown. She'd have to bid him goodbye without making a big deal out of it. Could she?

Well, of course she could. After she'd graduated from college and before starting her first job, she and some friends had spent the summer backpacking through Europe. They'd had an amazing time, but that trip had ended and the friends had scattered. They kept up through emails, but their summer of bonding was only a memory now.

Had she been sad when the trip had ended? Of course. Would she like the chance to do it again? Definitely. But that wasn't possible. Everyone's lives had taken different turns.

She vowed to think of this time with Luke that same way, minus the continued email connection. She doubted he'd want that. For the next few weeks, she'd pretend to be on vacation with Luke Griffin, her traveling companion on the road to sexual adventure.

Satisfied with her conclusions, she hurried toward the campsite. Fortunately it was as she'd left it. The tent was secure. After stowing her food supplies in a canvas sack attached to a pulley, she hoisted it out of bear reach. Then she opened the outside tent flaps to air it out and tucked her clean clothes in another canvas sack inside the tent.

At last she was ready to check on the eagles. With her computer, her camera and her binoculars in a smaller backpack, she climbed the ladder to her platform. Like an absent mother coming home to her children, she was eager to see what had happened to her charges while she'd been gone.

And like that same mother, when she looked through her binoculars and spotted the two nestlings, she was sure they appeared bigger than they had the day before. Her scientific self knew that one day wouldn't have made much of a difference. Yet they seemed to be moving around more. The larger of the two lifted its fuzzy head and looked in her direction.

"Hi there," she murmured with a smile. "Miss me?"

The nestling turned, giving her a profile view, and blinked.

"Someday you're going to be a magnificent eagle with a snowy head and talons strong enough to grip a small deer. I won't recognize you."

She wouldn't have any artificial means of tracking them, either. She agreed with the professor's decision not to use telemetry to keep tabs on these birds after they left the nest. Radio tracking could help researchers learn about the eagles' habits, but Naomi disliked anything that might interfere with their normal behavior.

Yet at times like these, when she felt a kinship with the creatures she'd been studying, she longed for a way to trace their journey after they left this meadow. She thought she'd be able to recognize the parents if they returned next spring. The male had a scar above his right eye, and the female was missing one toe on her left claw. But even if the babies came back here, too, they would have changed drastically by then.

Lowering the binoculars, she set up her folding table and camp stool. Then she turned on her computer and checked the webcam feed. She hadn't updated Professor Scranton recently, so she sent him a report and received an immediate and grateful response.

The guy could easily be in his nineties, and he had done his share of fieldwork in his day, but now health issues prevented him from doing the research for his paper. He'd told Naomi that her information provided the energy boost he needed to keep writing.

Even so, he'd urged her to take breaks and not neglect her normal life while observing the eagles. She'd assured him that at the moment, she didn't have a particularly exciting life and would be happy to spend most of her time focused on the nest and its occupants. Of course, that had been before Luke Griffin had ridden under her tree.

But Luke didn't want her to drop everything for him, even if she'd been so inclined. He actively *wanted* her to be involved in her career, because that guaranteed she wouldn't become needy. She began to see the sense in what he'd been trying to tell her. He was a man for the new breed of independent women, of which she was definitely one.

An eagle's shrill cry caught her attention. Raising her binoculars, she watched the female glide into the nest with another fish in her talons. Feeding time.

Naomi grabbed her digital camera and took several shots. Then, using the webcam image, she sat at her computer and made rapid notes.

After the female left the nest again, Naomi scanned the area with her binoculars for no particular reason, except…a feeling. Something about the scenery had changed. The more she'd worked in the wild, the more her senses had sharpened, so maybe she'd known he was coming even before he'd appeared.

Through the powerful lens she watched Luke riding toward her, exactly as he had the day before. He had the same relaxed style, and although his shirt was a different plaid than the one he'd worn yesterday, he looked very much the same. But nothing was the same.

She lowered her binoculars, unwilling to spy on him today. He was no longer a hot stranger to ogle as a distraction from her research duties. He was Luke, the man she'd agreed to have sex with. And he was coming for her.

LUKE RODE INTO the clearing and wondered if she was watching him through her binoculars. He couldn't remember ever starting an affair this way, where they'd discussed the issue and had come to the conclusion they'd go for it a good twelve hours before anything actually happened.

Usually the decision was made during a passionate make-out session, and there wasn't much logic involved until later. After they'd had wild sex, he would gently explain his position on commitment, and because he'd chosen wisely, the woman in his arms would thank him for not expecting anything permanent.

Everything was different with Naomi, probably because they'd met out here, under the blue Wyoming sky, and he was fascinated by the nature of her work. In the past he'd hooked up with business types who'd been looking for a hot cowboy in a country-and-western bar. That had to be the source of the difference. His other lovers had come looking for someone like him.

When he'd heard about Naomi's eagle research and her wildlife background, he'd been so intrigued that he'd made a point to connect with this interesting woman. That had put him in the unfamiliar position of trying to impress *her.* He seemed to have done a decent job so far. He couldn't speak for her anticipation level, but the twelve hours since they'd decided to become lovers had ramped up his libido considerably.

Still, he might want to add some style to his entrance. Slapping his hat against Smudge's rump, he urged the gelding into a gallop and cut across the meadow, heading straight for her tree.

He didn't dare look up to see how she was taking this frontal assault, because he had to keep his attention on the terrain. Racing toward her wasn't all that bright, perhaps, but it had chutzpah. A few yards shy of the platform, he reined in his horse in a spurt of dust.

Very showy, if he did say so. He kept a tight hold on Smudge, who was prancing and blowing like a stallion. Tilting his hat back with his thumb, he glanced up. "Howdy, ma'am." He might sound casual, but his heart was pounding like crazy.

"Howdy, yourself." Grinning, Naomi leaned over the railing. She looked adorable, with her hair in a high, flirty ponytail. "That was quite—"

"Stupid?"

"I was going to say dashing."

"Dashing." He squinted up at her. The sun created a halo around her blond hair, but he knew she was no angel. Desire tightened his groin. "That's what I was going for. Dashing."

"You achieved it. You looked like a Hollywood cowboy."

"You should see me twirl my lariat."

"I'd love to."

He couldn't seem to stop staring at her. The sunshine fell on her like a spotlight, turning her into a blonde princess. If he hadn't pushed his horse into a gallop on the way over here, he could have ground-tied him and ascended to the platform as any decent Hollywood cowboy would do.

As the ache for her grew, he longed to climb that ladder and claim his prize. But Smudge needed a cooldown. And while Luke was at it, he might as well settle the horse into his temporary quarters.

"Are you coming up or do you want me to come down?"

"I'll come up. Let me get Smudge sorted out first. How are the eagles?"

"Good. All seems to be well."

"Excellent. I'll be right back." He clicked his tongue and guided Smudge around the tree and over toward her campsite. After walking the horse around the campsite awhile, Luke dismounted.

He'd come prepared for the duration, with supplies in two bulging saddlebags. Unsaddling Smudge, he put the saddle, blanket and bags over by Naomi's tent. "Welcome to your home away from home, Smudge." He replaced the horse's bridle with a halter and led him down to the stream for a drink.

His promise to "be right back" might have been overly optimistic. Returning to the campsite, he tied Smudge to a tree while he found a good grazing area near the tent. Then he pulled a ground stake out of a saddlebag, along with a mallet, and planted the stake. Finally he transferred Smudge's lead rope from the tree to the stake.

That should take care of the horse until tonight, but he understood why Naomi chose to hike out here instead of riding. A horse was one more thing to deal with. Still, he had limited time to be with her, and even with these few chores, he'd saved valuable minutes by riding instead of hiking.

After scratching Smudge's neck and giving him a handful of carrots from his pocket, Luke walked down the path Naomi's hiking boots had created during her many treks. He couldn't remember the last time he'd been this excited about being with a woman.

He could easily guess why that was. Her interest in wildlife indicated that she was as interested in adventure and exploration as he was. At least she was now. He cautioned himself not to make assumptions of how she'd be in the future.

But he didn't care about the future. At this moment he had the green light to spend quality time with a woman who studied eagles. That would make everything more exciting, including the sex. He had condoms in his saddlebags and in his pocket. Life was good.

He'd look at the eagles first, because he really was interested in them, and because if he didn't look at them first, he might never get around to it. After he'd checked out the eagles, he intended to kiss Naomi until they both couldn't see straight. That dramatic race over here had made him feel like a conquering hero.

"Coming up!" He climbed the ladder and thought of Rapunzel. Naomi was also a blonde, but he appreciated being able to use a ladder instead of her braided hair to reach her tower.

"Hurry!" she said.

"Why?" He hoped it was because she couldn't wait to feel his hands on her.

"Both parents are there for feeding time! It's like a family portrait."

Luke smiled. She really dug those eagles, and he liked that about her. Any woman who was passionate about one thing had the capacity to be passionate about other things, too. He'd sensed that about Naomi from the beginning.

Once he reached the platform, he was struck again by the spectacular view. This platform would be an awesome place to watch the sunset. He'd keep that in mind for later.

She glanced over at him, her color high. "Here." She took off her binoculars. "Take a look."

"Thanks." He accepted the binoculars, but he couldn't resist cupping the back of her head and giving her a quick kiss. "Hi."

"Hi." She sounded breathless.

That was good. She would be even more breathless before long. Adrenaline rushed through his veins. Eagles and a hot woman. What could be better than that?

"I think the nestlings have grown a little." She came to stand next to him. "Tell me what you think."

With her standing so close and radiating warmth and the tantalizing scent of arousal, he couldn't think very well at all. But he made a valiant attempt. Lifting the binoculars, he focused on the nest.

To his surprise, he did notice a difference, even if it was slight. "They're growing, especially the bully. Look at that little sucker, shoving the other one out of the way. C'mon, you. Let the little one have some food."

She chuckled. "So you root for the underdog?"

"Doesn't everybody?" Between having her right beside him and the incredible view of the eagles, he was on sensory overload.

"Humans often do. We're at the top of the food chain, so we can afford to worry about the weak link. Wild animals don't always have that luxury."

"Good point." Luke desperately wanted to slide one arm around her and pull her close, but he knew what that would lead to. Once he touched her, there would be no eagle watching going on.

"Most of the time they're focused on survival." Naomi sighed. "They're so vulnerable."

"You mean the babies?"

"And the parents."

He focused on the sharp beaks and strong talons of the male and female eagles. "They look so powerful."

"I know. But all it takes is a shortage of food, or a car windshield, or an electrical wire, or a gun. We nearly wiped them out."

"Thank God we didn't. Now people are into watching them instead of shooting them."

"Which means I'm employed. That reminds me that I need to make some notes. Can you keep track of the feeding session and report what's happening while I type?"

"Sure." He missed her warmth the second she moved away to sit at her folding table, but he couldn't forget that she had a job to do. That's why he'd planned to stay overnight. She wouldn't be watching the eagles once darkness fell.

He hoped she'd go along with the plan. Now that he thought about it, he wondered if he should have checked with her first. They'd been hot for each other last night, and he was still burning, but she might have cooled down since then.

Well, he'd find out soon enough. In the meantime, he'd act as her research assistant, which wasn't a bad deal. In fact, he considered it a privilege to be involved, even a little bit, in her work.

"After they leave the nest, will you have any way of tracking what happens to them?"

The steady click of the keys stopped for a moment. "No. I won't be banding them. It's too invasive."

"I agree." He went back to describing the movements of the eagles, and she continued to type.

Then she paused again. "I take it you got the afternoon off?"

"Yes, I did. Okay, it looks like the father is getting ready to leave the nest."

She started typing again. "When do you have to go back?" The keys clicked rhythmically.

"Tomorrow morning."

Her typing came to an abrupt halt.

Although his back was to her, he swore he could feel the intensity of her stare. Suddenly it seemed several degrees warmer on the platform. "If that's okay with you."

Behind him, the laptop closed with a soft snap.

"I won't interfere with your work." Lowering the binoculars, he turned around, hoping he hadn't misjudged, hoping he would find… *Yes.* The same emotion sizzling in his veins heated her blue gaze. His pulse hammered as he held that gaze.

Slowly she stood. When she drew in a breath, her body quivered. "Interfere with my work." She stepped out from behind the small table. "Please."

6

Ever since Luke had come charging toward her across the meadow, Naomi had felt like a shaken bottle of champagne ready to blow at any second. Intellectually she'd known that leaping from his horse and scaling the platform would be silly, but her romantic heart had wanted him to do that all the same. She'd wanted to be taken in a mad rush of passion that gave her no time to think.

But he'd taken freaking *forever* to deal with his horse, which was a good thing but didn't scream eagerness on his part. So she'd concluded he was here as much to see the eagles as to see her, especially after he'd mentioned them before he'd ridden over to the campsite.

But now…now he looked the way she felt. His throat moved in a quick swallow. "How sturdy is this platform, anyway?"

Her heart rate climbed. "Sturdy enough, but—" She

thought of the logistics. Both of them were wearing complicated clothing.

"Right. We're both way overdressed for this."

"We are." She thought longingly of her transparent nightgown and the entrance she could make if they were in a hotel room instead of on a wooden platform twenty feet above the ground. Instead she wore extremely unsexy hiking shorts, a T-shirt and, most problematic of all, hiking boots.

No man should be forced to remove his lover's lace-up hiking boots before they had sex. So that meant she needed to undress herself. Then she thought of what fun it would be to watch Luke strip down right here on her observation platform. Anybody could make a luxury suite seem seductive, but how many people could say they'd had sex in a tree?

She turned and grabbed her camp stool. "I don't know about you, but I'm going to slip into something more comfortable."

A slow smile made him look even more breathtakingly handsome. He took off his hat and laid it brim-side up on the platform. "I knew we were going to get along."

"That's a different hat." She unlaced her boot and pulled it off along with her sock.

"Sarah's going to see what she can do with the other one." He unsnapped his cuffs as he watched her pull off her other boot. "But if you ask me, one ruined hat is a small price to pay."

Her body tingled from the gleam in his eyes. "You don't know that yet."

"Yes, I do." He unsnapped his shirt.

"I might be lousy at sex."

He laughed.

"Really, I might. You know that underdog syndrome we talked about?" She stood and the wood felt warm under her bare feet. "Those are the guys I tend to pick."

"So I'm an underdog? Ouch!" He pulled off his shirt and dropped it to the platform.

"Oh, no." Her gaze traveled lovingly over his broad chest. "You're no underdog."

"That's a relief." He sent her a sizzling glance as his hands went to his belt buckle. "Better get moving, Perkins. You're falling behind."

"No, I'm not." But she'd been caught standing motionless and staring. She'd admit that. "You still have your boots on."

"So I do." He paused, his fingers at the button of his jeans. "After you take off your shirt, how about tossing that stool over here?"

"I can do it now." She reached for it.

"Please pull off your shirt," he said softly. "Your boots seemed to take forever. I thought I'd go crazy."

She paused. Until now she'd been so focused on him that she'd forgotten that he might be as eager to watch her undress. "Don't expect sexy underwear," she said.

"Why would you wear sexy underwear when you're camping?"

With a smile, she echoed his earlier comment. "I knew we'd get along." Then she grabbed her T-shirt and yanked it over her head.

"Mmm."

His murmur of approval sent heat flooding through her, and moisture gathered between her thighs.

"More." His voice sounded husky. "The bra, too."

She trembled as excitement warred with her natural modesty. "I've never stripped for a man in broad daylight."

"I'm honored to be the first." His chest expanded as he dragged in a breath and let it out slowly. His glance was hungry. "Come on, Naomi. I want to see you with sunlight on your breasts."

Pulse hammering, she reached behind her back and unfastened the hooks of her white cotton bra. Then she drew it off and let it fall to the platform.

His gaze held hers for a few seconds before dipping. Then it returned to lock with hers. His voice was tight. "You're incredible. And I want to touch you more than I want to breathe."

Her nipples tightened and she quivered with longing. "Then touch me."

With a groan of surrender, he eliminated the space between them and crushed her in a fierce embrace. Bare skin met the solid wall of his chest, and she gasped at the pleasure of that first contact.

"I need you so much." His mouth found hers as he pulled her in close, letting her feel the hard ridge beneath the fly of his jeans.

The urgency of his kiss drove her wild. No man had ever wanted her like this, as if he couldn't contain the passion gripping him. Keeping her firmly wedged against his crotch, he continued kissing her as he leaned back enough to cup her breast in one large hand. His moan of need vibrated through her.

His hands were calloused from his work, and that only made his touch more erotic. She squirmed against him, aching for relief from the tension that tightened with each thrust of his tongue into her mouth and squeeze of his hand on her breast.

Desperation drove her to shove her hand between them and unfasten the button on his jeans. As she began working the zipper down, he lifted away from her, giving her access. When she slipped her hand inside his briefs and wrapped her fingers around the silky power of his cock, he began to shake.

He lifted his mouth from hers and gulped for air. "I'm going insane."

She moaned as his thumb brushed her nipple. "Me, too."

"We have to… We're not…"

"Condom. Do you…?"

"Yes, but I haven't…my boots are still…"

Her fevered brain searched for the quickest way for them to achieve their goal. "The stool."

"Oh." He let her go long enough to find the stool and grab it.

She used that time to get out of her shorts and soaked panties. When she turned back to him, he was sitting on the stool pulling off his boots, and he held the condom packet in his teeth.

"Forget the boots."

The one he'd been holding fell from his hand with a clatter as she stood before him, trembling with urges stronger than she'd ever had in her life. Those urges made her bold.

"Put on the condom." She braced her hands on his broad shoulders.

His breathing ragged, he quickly did as she asked.

"Now…" She gripped his shoulders. "Help me down."

Hands at her waist, he looked into her eyes as he supported her slow descent.

She felt the nudge of his cock.

Lightning flashed in his brown eyes. He shifted slightly, found her moist entrance. "You're drenched."

"Your fault."

"Hope so." His jaw muscles flexed as he drew her down.

Her fingers dug into his shoulders and she moaned softly.

"Too much?"

She shook her head, unable to speak as he took her deeper and touched off tiny explosions all the way down. So this was what they wrote books and songs about. Now she knew what she'd been missing.

At last she was settled on his lap, her feet on the platform, her body gearing up for what promised to be a spectacular and imminent orgasm. The advance-warning signals rippled through her, making her gulp.

He continued to hold her gaze, but his jaw muscles tensed even more, making the cords of his neck stand out. Sweat glistened on his powerful chest. "Don't move." He shuddered. "I don't want to come yet."

But she couldn't control what her body craved. An involuntary spasm rocked her.

He sucked in a breath and squeezed his eyes shut. "Don't."

"Can't...help it."

Slowly he opened his eyes again, and a wry smile touched his mouth. "You're potent."

"You, too." Another spasm hit.

He swallowed. "Okay, if that's going to keep happening, we might as well go for it."

"Yes, please."

"Oh, Naomi." Laughter and lust sparkled in his eyes. "I had no clue." He drew in a shaky breath. "Ride me, lady. Ride me."

She did, and it was a very short ride. She came almost immediately, gasping with the wonder of it, and he followed two strokes later with a groan wrenched from deep inside him. Quivering in the aftermath, she leaned her forehead against his damp shoulder and listened to the labored rasp of his breathing.

A soft breeze sighed through the pine needles and brushed against her skin. Gradually she became aware of small birds chattering and the rustle of a squirrel in the branches somewhere nearby. She'd always felt a part of nature, but never more so than at this moment.

Luke gently massaged the back of her neck. "That was quite a beginning."

"Uh-huh." She wondered if sex was always this good for him, but she wouldn't ask. "Am I too heavy?"

"Light as a feather." He ran a hand up her back. "Soft as satin."

"I suppose we'll have to move sometime."

"Definitely. Especially if we want to do this again in the near future."

She lifted her head to stare at him. "How near in the future?"

He grinned at her. "That was just a warm-up." He gazed into her eyes. "Am I shocking you, Naomi Perkins?"

She didn't want to admit that she'd never been with a guy who suggested more sex immediately after having it. Apparently she really had been choosing from the shallow end of the gene pool, picking underdogs with a low sex drive.

"We don't have to have sex in the near future," he murmured. "If you need more time, we can wait."

"I don't need more time, but I thought that you, being a guy, would."

"If I weren't starving to death, I'd be ready to go in about ten minutes, but I'm hungry. Are you?"

She hadn't given herself a chance to think about it, but she'd skipped lunch. "Yes, I'm hungry, but I'm all set with my energy drinks and a few munchies. I doubt that you—"

"You've got that right. I brought food enough for both of us, so save your energy drinks for when I'm not here. That way there's no danger of history repeating itself."

"I wouldn't spill it on you again, I promise."

"You never know." He traced the outline of her mouth with the tip of his finger. "You could be drinking one of those green concoctions, be hit with the sudden need to have sex with me and knock the bottle over in your hurry to rip my clothes off."

She laughed. "That's pretty far-fetched." In reality, it wasn't, but she had to be careful not to let him know how powerfully he affected her.

"So you say, but please humor me and don't open one of those while I'm here, okay?"

"Do they carry a bad association for you, then?"

"Actually, no. It's a good association, but even so, I don't care to repeat it. The energy drink served a purpose by bringing us together, so I'm done with it." He gave her a quick kiss. "Let's disengage and I'll head back to the campsite and fetch our lunch."

"Okay." She eased away from him and stood. "FYI, there's a little garbage bag over by the cooler."

"Thanks."

She walked to the far side of the platform to give him some privacy to deal with the condom. How odd that she wasn't embarrassed about strolling around the platform naked. At least she wasn't until she saw a rider at the far edge of the clearing. "Yikes. Someone's coming." She scrambled for her clothes.

"You're kidding." Luke zipped his pants. "Damn it. Where did I set the binoculars?"

"On the table. You'd better put on your shirt." She scurried around getting her clothes back on. Fortunately they always looked rumpled. She used the stool to balance as she put on her socks and hiking boots. That stool would always have the memory of what they'd used it for today.

Luke peered through the binoculars. “It’s Jack. And he’s got little Archie in the saddle with him.”

“Oh.” Naomi felt silly for not remembering. “That’s my fault. I told him to bring Archie to see the eagles sometime.”

“And he picked today. I wonder if that’s pure coincidence.” Luke put down the binoculars and picked up his shirt. “Emmett’s supposed to be the only one who knows I’m out here with you.”

“So you talked to him?” She took the elastic out of her hair and redid her ponytail.

“Last night on the way home.” Luke buttoned his shirt and tucked it into his jeans. “He reluctantly accepted the idea that you and I would be hanging out together during my time off.”

“Then it’s probably coincidence that Jack decided to come out today.” She was grateful that she hadn’t been wearing makeup. She turned toward Luke. “How do I look?”

He smiled. “Like a woman who’s been up to no good.”

“Really? What’s different about me? Is my mouth red?”

“A little, but not much.” He rolled back the sleeves of his shirt instead of fastening the cuffs.

“Doggone it.”

“Hey.” He took her by the shoulders. “I was kidding you. You look fine. I’m probably the only one who would notice a postorgasmic gleam in your eye.”

“Luke! I don’t want to have a gleam in my eye!”

“Sorry. You probably can’t do anything about it.

I'm pretty good at detecting that gleam, but most people aren't."

"I'll bet Jack is. Before he married Josie, he was quite the ladies' man. I wish I had a mirror."

"Trust me, you look fine. That's not what's going to get us in trouble."

She stared at him. "What's going to get us in trouble?"

"I unsaddled my horse and took the time to stake him out in a grazing area. A short visit wouldn't have required all that. I would have left Smudge ground-tied beside this tree."

Naomi groaned. "Then I guess we'll have to see what kind of reaction Jack has to that. He's not a blabbermouth, so maybe this won't get back to my folks."

"Yeah, Emmett said they wouldn't like it."

"Only because they want me to find a guy who's steady. That's not you."

"Nope. Not me."

The sound of hoofbeats grew louder. Naomi glanced at Luke. "We could sit down against the tree and pretend we're not here."

"Like you tried to do with me?"

"Right."

"Forget it. If Jack brought his son all the way out here to see the eagles, he'd haul him up on this platform even if he thought nobody was here. Then he'd find us hiding and looking guilty as hell."

"You're right. That would be embarrassing."

"And because we've stood here debating the issue

for too long, there's no time for me to climb down and disappear into the woods."

That made her laugh. "Hardly. Even if you made it down the ladder, you couldn't get away without Jack hearing you sneaking away through the trees. That would be just as bad as staying here and facing the music."

"At least we're dressed. And we're not actually in the midst of—"

"Oh, God." She put her hands to her hot cheeks. "What if he'd ridden up twenty minutes ago?"

"Little Archie would have gotten an education." Luke shrugged. "He's a ranch kid. He needs to understand the facts of life."

"He's only two," she said in an undertone. "He doesn't need to understand anything yet." She took a calming breath. "This could have been so much worse. I'm grateful that it wasn't."

"Naomi!" Jack's deep baritone drifted upward. "You there?"

She walked to the edge of the platform. "Hi, Jack! I sure am. Hi, Archie!"

The little blond toddler waved wildly. "Hi, hi! Birds! See birds!" He didn't look much like his dark-haired, dark-eyed father. Instead he'd inherited his fair coloring from his mother, Josie.

He was an adorable kid, beloved by his parents, aunts and uncles and grandparents. Naomi's heart did a little flip-flop. No matter what awkwardness the situation produced, this child deserved to see the eagles.

He was very young, but even early memories could have a lasting impression, if only in his subconscious.

"Come on up," she called. "I have a surprise for you. Luke's here."

Jack tipped back his hat and gazed up at her. "Oh, is he, now?"

Archie bounced on the saddle. "Luke! Wanna see Luke!"

Luke joined her at the edge of the platform. "Hey, buddy! How're you doing?"

"Luke!" Archie stretched his arms up. "Wanna see Luke!"

"We'll be right there," Jack said. "Make sure the eagles are ready for their close-up." He dropped his reins, gripped Archie around his chubby middle and dismounted.

"Archie seems excited to see you," Naomi said quietly.

"I've done some babysitting now and then."

She glanced over at him. The drifter babysat for little children? That didn't fit his supposed philosophy of not becoming attached to his surroundings. Little kids like Archie could grab hold of your heart and refuse to let go. "You're a man of many parts."

"I am." He gave her a cocky smile and lowered his voice. "After they leave, I'll show you some of them."

7

FROM THE MOMENT Jack arrived on the platform, Luke knew that he'd come to check out the situation brewing with Naomi. Jack was easing into the role of reigning monarch of the Last Chance, despite the fact he wasn't yet forty. But he considered everyone on the ranch, and most of the people in town, too, as his people—people who required his guidance.

Luke had found it kind of amusing until today. Yes, Jack was his boss, and technically what happened on his property was under his control, but… Okay, maybe Jack had some authority here. Luke didn't have to like it.

Archie, though, was another story. Luke couldn't resist that rosy-cheeked little boy. He dragged the stool over to a spot that would give Archie the best view of the eagles and sat with the kid on his lap and helped him look through the binoculars. It was tricky because Archie didn't quite get the concept of the binoculars.

Luke had a little trouble managing both child and

binoculars. He didn't want to drop either one, with the kid being the more important of the two.

Naomi came to his rescue. "You hold Archie, and I'll hold the binoculars."

"Wanna hold nockles!" Archie stubbornly refused to give up his right to have a hand on them, even if he didn't quite understand how they worked.

"Okay," Naomi said. "We'll all hold them. You, me and Luke."

"'Kay." Archie settled down.

Naomi crouched down next to them. "Archie, can you make your fingers do this?" She created two circles with her thumbs and forefingers and held them up to her eyes.

Archie imitated her, which meant he had to let go of the binoculars, but Luke made sure they didn't drop.

"That's how the binoculars work," Naomi said. "Like your fingers, only better."

Jack observed from the sidelines. "Brilliant."

"We'll see." Naomi had Archie practice with his fingers some more, and then she tried the binoculars again. Eventually Archie caught on.

Once he did, he was very excited. "Birds! I see birds!"

Luke held him as he bounced, but Archie kept his eyes pressed against the twin lenses. Glancing over at Naomi, Luke discovered her looking back at him. They exchanged a smile.

He had a brief flash of what it would be like to be a dad teaching his kid how to use binoculars for the first time. He'd always assumed that whenever he wanted a kid fix, he'd borrow one, like now. But being able to share this kind of moment on a regular basis had its appeal, especially if the other person in the equation happened to be a woman like Naomi.

Then he corrected himself. Not someone *like* Naomi, because he'd already determined that she was one of a kind. It would have to be Naomi herself. He was thinking crazy. He'd been over this ground and knew what he wanted out of life. Absolute and complete freedom.

Being a father came at a stiff price. His own father had made no secret of that. At a young age, Luke had asked for a baby sister or brother. Luke's dad had rolled his eyes and proclaimed that one kid was more than enough to take care of. Luke had never forgotten his father's martyred expression.

Luke could have fun on a temporary basis with other people's kids, like Archie. The little boy had a fairly long attention span for his age, but when the thrill was gone, it was totally gone. Luke handed the binoculars to Naomi and stood up, hoisting Archie into his arms.

Archie wiggled in protest. "Wanna get down!"

"That's my cue," Jack said. "Time to get this guy home. Can't have him running around on a platform twenty feet in the air."

"Great job on the platform," Luke said. "It's plenty sturdy."

"Glad to hear it." Jack continued to eye Luke with suspicion. "How about helping me get Archie down the ladder? Climbing up is much easier. I'd appreciate it if you'd go down and hold it steady at the bottom."

"Will do." It was a reasonable request, but Luke

couldn't help thinking there was an ulterior motive involved.

Sure enough, when Jack reached the bottom safely with Archie on his hip, he turned to Luke and lowered his voice. "What's going on with you and Naomi?"

Luke glanced up toward the platform. He wasn't sure how well sound carried. "We're attracted to each other, and we're both consenting adults."

"I figured something like that."

"Did Emmett say anything?"

"No, he didn't." Jack speared Luke with a glance. "Is he aware of this?"

"He is. I talked to him last night. He said I could ride Smudge over here."

"That reminds me. You were at the Spirits and Spurs with Emmett last night. What was your take on this Clifford Mason guy?"

"Dresses like a rhinestone cowboy, but other than that, I know nothing about him. Emmett's not happy that Pam went to dinner with him."

"She did that because she's the main sponsor of the town's Fourth of July spectacular. Mason is providing the fireworks, and Pam's paying for them."

"Does Emmett know that?"

"He does now, because I told him. I also told him that rumor has it the guy is interested in Pam. He didn't take that well. So FYI, he's not in the best of moods."

"Thanks for the warning. I'll watch myself. He's not totally in favor of my coming out here, so if he's upset about something else besides…" Luke sighed. "I'll just be careful."

"Do that. Look, I don't care what you do on your own time, for the most part, but Naomi is a great person, and you've made it clear you're leaving."

"She knows that. She's fine with it."

"Okay." Jack didn't sound as if he believed it.

"Wanna go home." Archie laid his head on Jack's shoulder.

"I know you have to head back, but I have a question." Luke could see Archie was fading. He needed his nap. "If Emmett didn't say anything about me coming to see Naomi, how did you figure out what was going on?"

"Mom asked me if I had any ideas about cleaning your hat. I know Naomi's big on that green glop, and when I realized that was the liquid that had ruined your hat, I put two and two together."

"My hat's ruined?"

"It's ruined, bro. You can't treat a good hat that way and expect it to survive." Jack looked rather cheerful delivering the news.

"Sorry to hear that." Luke decided not to point out that Naomi had been the one to spill the energy drink on his hat. He'd had nothing to do with the accident. Oh, well. He'd resigned himself to this loss, but that didn't make him happy to hear the hat was DOA.

"Just so you know, if you break Naomi's heart, more than your hat is in jeopardy."

"I've been completely honest with her, Jack. She knows I don't intend to settle down."

Jack gazed at him. "If you say so. But she's one of

ours. And you're not." He touched the brim of his hat. "See you back at the ranch."

As Jack walked away and mounted up, Luke ran a hand over his face. *She's one of ours. And you're not.* That was true, and it was his choice. He'd never been part of any group, and he'd liked it that way.

So why did Jack's words sting? He didn't want to be tied down to this community, or to any community, for that matter. Sure, Jack had a close family, a loving wife and a cute kid, but they all came at the price of his freedom. Jack couldn't pick up and leave whenever he wanted to. He had obligations.

Knowing that, Luke shouldn't be affected by the dire warning Jack had thrown out. The guy's threats were empty and meaningless to someone like Luke. They shouldn't have any effect on him whatsoever.

And they wouldn't. He knew who he was and what he wanted out of life. Many people didn't, and they stumbled along without a plan, allowing circumstances to dictate their future. He wasn't like that.

He waited until Jack and Archie rode away. Then he called up to the platform. "Still want some lunch?"

Naomi came to the top of the ladder. "More than ever. I'm famished." She hesitated. "Did Jack give you a talking-to?"

"Oh, yeah. He and Emmett are both worried that I'm going to break your heart. But Jack was more direct. He promised if I broke your heart, he'd break my legs. Or something to that effect."

"Good grief! Don't these guys realize I can take care of myself?"

"Apparently not."

"I find that rather patronizing…but sort of sweet, too."

Luke took note of that. She might not like being considered a fragile flower in need of protection from men like him, but she didn't mind having representatives from the community watching out for her, either. He'd be wise not to criticize either Emmett or Jack for their behavior. Naomi loved them both and was flattered that they cared enough to stick up for her, even if it wasn't required.

But she'd welcomed Luke to her hideaway, and he'd had one hell of a time with her until Jack had shown up. Despite Jack's obvious scrutiny of their arrangement, Naomi hadn't told Luke to go away. She, at least, didn't think Luke was taking unfair advantage of her. In fact, he'd be shortchanging her if he let Jack's visit cast a pall over the celebration.

He gazed up at her. "I'll be back in a flash with some food."

"Sounds great."

"If you feel like taking off your hiking boots, don't let me stop you."

She laughed, as he'd hoped she would. Then she blew him a kiss and moved away from the edge of the platform. Yeah, they would get their groove back. Jack Chance wasn't going to rain on their parade.

Within fifteen minutes, he had a feast spread out on the platform. He'd even brought a tablecloth, which impressed Naomi to no end.

"Pretty fancy for camping, Griffin." She sat on the

far side of the checkered cloth he'd spread out on the platform. And she was, happy day, barefoot.

"You're camping, but I rode in on a horse, so I can provide more luxuries." He was proud of the cheese, cold cuts and sliced bakery bread he'd brought for making sandwiches. Shoshone's little grocery store wasn't huge, but it carried quality stuff. He'd included only mustard because mayonnaise didn't keep as well.

"This is wonderful." Naomi took one of the paper plates he'd provided and made a sandwich.

Luke waited until she was finished before putting his together. "I considered bringing wine, but I didn't want to sabotage your eagle research, so I brought sparkling water instead. Which reminds me, do you need to check on the birds?"

"After we finish lunch. The webcam does the bulk of the work, but someone should be monitoring the nest on a regular basis and taking some digital still shots. The professor gets the constant webcam feed, but he makes good use of my personal notes and the stills, too."

"How did you hook up with him?"

"He put an ad in the paper, and out of all the people who answered it, he picked me."

"Of course he would." Luke was quickly becoming her biggest fan. "You have the credentials and you're extremely personable. I'm surprised you haven't landed a job with one of the national parks yet."

"Everyone has budget issues, and I'm relatively new to the profession. The parks are struggling to keep their veterans employed, and that's what they should do. I can wait it out. I don't have lots of bills, and I can stay with my folks and pay a small amount of rent. I also have some savings."

He nodded. "You're like me. I don't worry if I don't have a job right this minute, because I know I'll find something eventually. Whereas my dad got a job with an electronics company right out of college and never left. He thinks if he did, no one else would hire him."

"And you don't want to live in fear like that," she said.

"God, no. Fear makes you afraid to take risks." He bit into his sandwich. It was about a thousand times better than her energy drink.

"Have you ever been engaged?"

Now, there was a question right out of left field. She should know that he wouldn't do that. "I'm not into marriage." He glanced at her. "How about you?"

"A guy asked me once, but I couldn't see him as the father of my children. So I said no, but I did my best to be gentle about it."

"So that's your criteria? A guy has to pass muster as the future father of your children?"

"Well, I need to love him passionately, and we need a good sex life, but yeah, I'd want to be able to picture him as my future children's dad. Animals in the wild use that yardstick all the time and it's not a bad one."

She sure wouldn't consider a wanderer like him as a viable father of her kids, which was a good thing, really. "I take it you are planning to have kids, then."

She laughed. "I'm planning and my parents are

praying. I'm an only child, so if they're going to have grandchildren to spoil, I'm their only hope."

He was also an only child. His mother had made some noises about grandkids, but his dad had cautioned him to live his life for himself and not worry about providing grandchildren. Luke had heard the unspoken message—*don't make my mistakes.*

Naomi gazed at him. "Did you think I wouldn't want kids?"

"I don't see how you'd manage a family and still be so involved with wild-animal research."

"People do manage it. There's a woman who took her little boy out on the boat while she studied whales. If I could get a job at Yellowstone, then being married and having a family would be no problem at all because it's so close to Shoshone. My folks would help when they could, and I know a bunch of people around here. Child care would be a breeze because I'd have a support system."

He stared at her as a million contradictory thoughts battled in his head. "That kind of thinking is so foreign to me. I've never thought in terms of having a support system." He was both attracted and repelled by the concept.

Something that looked dangerously like pity flickered in her blue eyes. Then it was gone. "If you're a really strong person, I guess you don't need one. When I was in Florida, I had friends, and I cobbled together a loose kind of support system. But it wasn't anything like I have here."

"So does that mean you feel tied to this place?" He was still sorting it out.

"Not at all. In fact, it's the opposite. Let's say I did get a job around here, found the right guy, had a couple of kids. And then I had some fabulous research opportunity for a few weeks. Being here would mean I could consider it, because I'd have backup. Backup in addition to my husband, of course, whoever he might be. I'd have other people I could count on, too."

"I don't know." He shook his head. "It seems a little too cozy for me."

"I'm sure it does. You're a lone wolf. I shouldn't describe this as a one-way street, either. If I expect to count on others to help me, then when they need backup, I have to make myself available."

"Aha." He knew there had to be a catch. "So you could end up being tied down by them."

"For a little while. It's supposed to even out. If I ask my parents to babysit, then I have to be willing to watch their house and feed their dog if they go on vacation. It's a trade-off."

Luke shuddered. "I couldn't deal with that."

"Then it's a good thing you've created the life that you have, isn't it?"

He met her gaze across the tablecloth, littered with the remains of their lunch. "Yes. I like it." He allowed himself a slow perusal of Naomi Perkins, from her bare toes to her golden ponytail. He and Naomi might be headed down different paths, but right now, they occupied the same place and time. "I'll tell you what else I like."

Her skin had turned a sweet shade of pink as he'd studied her. "What's that?"

"The idea of you naked on this tablecloth."

Her breath hitched. "That's quite a change of subject."

"We needed one." He started moving the food off the red checkered cloth. "All this talk about family ties and obligations was playing hell with my sex drive."

"Is that why you're such a sexy guy? You don't get involved in all that cozy family stuff?"

"You tell me." He pulled off his boots.

"Could be. You're a wild guy, Luke." Rising to her knees, she stripped off her T-shirt for the second time today.

And for the second time today, he drank in the sight of her undressing for him. "That must be why you like me." He unsnapped his shirt and took it off. "You're attracted to wild things."

"That's part of it." She gave him the same sort of once-over he'd given her and smiled. "Mostly I just want your body."

Lust shot straight to his groin. "Likewise." He lost track of his own undressing when she arched her back and reached for the clasp of her bra.

Snap, it came undone, and she pulled it off by the straps before tossing it aside. The motion made her breasts quiver. He became completely absorbed in watching them as she moved. When she unfastened her shorts and slid them, along with her panties, down to her knees, he had a visual feast.

He couldn't imagine ever growing tired of this

view—her pale, full breasts tipped with wine-dark nipples, her slender waist and the gentle curve of her hips. She would put an hourglass to shame. His glance traveled lower, to those blond curls covering what was currently his favorite place in the world.

"Now who's falling behind?" She rid herself of her shorts and panties, and her breasts jiggled again, capturing both his attention and his fevered imagination.

"I can't concentrate when you're doing that."

She gave him a saucy look. "I'm only following instructions."

"Then here's another one." He stood and unfastened his jeans. "Take your hair down."

"Okay." She lifted her hands to her ponytail.

"Stop."

"But you said—"

"I know, but I just want to look at you for a minute like that, kneeling on the tablecloth, your hands in your hair. You look like a wood nymph."

"Don't they usually wear clothes?" She pulled the elastic out of her hair and laid it on her pile of clothes.

"Not in my fantasy." He shucked his jeans and briefs while she combed out her shining hair with her fingers. He'd never thought he had a preference for a woman's coloring. But surely nothing was more beautiful than blond hair filled with sunlight.

"And there's my fantasy." She focused on his jutting cock. "Come closer." She ran her tongue over her lips. "I have a taste for something wild."

The blood roared in his ears as he walked toward her. Oh, yes, this was going to be good. Very good.

8

DRIVEN BY URGES she'd never had before, Naomi boldly wrapped both hands around his rigid penis. Until today, she'd never been naked with a man outdoors in broad daylight, and she'd certainly never done *this* out in the open, under a clear blue sky and a warm sun.

Holding him felt like clutching a lightning rod. Energy coursed between them, and her pulse rate skyrocketed. Glancing up, she looked into eyes filled with primitive fire. For this moment, he was truly a wild creature, and so was she.

Slowly she leaned forward. She began with her tongue, and he gasped. She wanted to make him gasp and groan and abandon himself to her questing mouth. Glorying in his salty taste, silky texture and blood-warmed strength, she accepted all he had to offer. The blunt tip brushed the back of her throat, and he trembled.

Then she began to move, applying suction here, a swirl of her tongue there, until his breathing grew labored. He slid his fingers through her hair and pressed them against her head. Another strangled moan was followed by his rapid breathing.

Her heart beat frantically as his excitement fueled hers. She sucked harder, and he cried out. His fingers pressed into her scalp and his body shook. When she was certain he was going to come, he tightened his hold and pulled back, out of reach. "No." He struggled to breathe. "No. I want—"

Quivering, he dropped to his knees. Still holding her head, he gave her an openmouthed kiss. His tongue dived into the warm recesses where his cock had been. But he didn't have the breath to kiss her for long.

He raised his head and looked into her eyes. "Let's do that…again…sometime."

"Anytime."

He smiled and massaged her scalp as his breathing grew steadier. "You may regret that."

"Never." Loving him that way, here on this open platform, had been wonderfully freeing. She vibrated with the power of it. She felt as if she could fly.

"Don't go away."

"Not a chance." She waited while he retrieved a condom from his jeans pocket. "Let me put it on."

He laughed. "Not yet." He tossed the packet next to the tablecloth and met her gaze. "First, I intend to taste the wildness in you, Naomi Perkins."

Ah. The air whooshed right out of her and liquid heat surged right in.

"Lie down," he murmured, his voice as soft and sexy as black velvet. "It's my turn to play."

She wondered if he could simply talk her into a climax with words spoken like that. The man knew his way around a seduction. She didn't care where or how he'd learned to make a woman melt like wax before a flame, as long as he kept that flame burning.

As she stretched out on the smooth cotton, she imagined herself a lioness on the African veld. Nothing covered her but the sky. And now, caressing her with his mouth and tongue, a powerful male was about to make her roar.

That roar began with a whimper as he touched her in secret places, sensitive places, erotic places. She writhed under the teasing lap of his tongue and the urgent tug of his teeth. His mouth was everywhere, exploring her with the thoroughness of a mapmaker.

And then…then came the most intimate touch of all. He tasted her with slow sips at first, but gradually his demanding tongue grew more self-assured. Spreading her thighs, he lifted her, creating the angle that he needed to take her in the most thorough, uncompromising kiss of them all.

His intent was clear, his pursuit of her orgasm relentless. She surrendered, arching against the determined thrust of his tongue and crying out as the spasms rocked her.

She was still riding the crest of that climax when he lowered her gently. Cool air touched her heated body for a moment before he was back, hovering over her, seeking, finding and driving deep.

She gasped and opened her eyes. He was there, gazing down at her, his expression fierce.

Leaning down, he bestowed a flavored kiss on her trembling lips. "You—" he eased back "—are…*magnificent.*" And he shoved home once more.

She looked into his dark eyes, clutched his hips and rose to meet his next stroke. Yes, she was magnificent—magnificently alive. She was bursting with energy and willing to dare…anything, even making love on an open platform twenty feet off the ground in the middle of the day.

"You're going to come again."

Her laughter was breathless. "Is that an order?"

"A promise." He shifted his angle slightly and increased the tempo.

Oh, yes. That would do it. The sweet friction had been wonderful before, but now he'd found the key to unlock her personal treasure chest. Her muted cries grew louder the faster he pumped.

"That's it." He began to pant. "I can feel you squeezing. Let go… There!"

He'd known it a split second before she had, but when her climax arrived, she yelled as she'd never yelled and she hung on tight as the swirling, tumbling force flung her into a brilliant realm of dazzling sensations.

She lost track of where she was, but she never lost track of who was with her. Luke—a god imbued with amazing powers. He'd given her pleasures she'd only dreamed of.

He didn't stop for her, nor would she have wanted him to. His thrusts prolonged the intensity, and when he came, his bellow of satisfaction vibrated through her, too. Then she absorbed his shudders as they blended with the aftershocks of her release. It was perfect sex. She might never have it again, but at least she'd had it once in her life, thanks to Luke Griffin.

She had no idea how long they lay there before he stirred.

Moving slowly, he propped himself on his forearms to gaze at her. "Wow."

She considered making a smart remark to lighten the mood, but he truly did look blown away. "Wow is right."

He smiled. "This was better than the stool."

"Think of what we could accomplish on an actual bed."

"Boggles the mind, doesn't it? I don't know, though. Being up in this tree house gives the whole experience a certain something."

"It's not boring."

"No." He dipped his head and kissed her softly. He added more kisses to her cheeks, her eyes and her nose. "But I have trouble imagining anything being boring with you."

"Coming from a man who treasures variety, that's quite a compliment."

He looked into her eyes again. "I meant it to be. That's probably what brought me out here yesterday. I couldn't imagine how a woman who studies eagles from a platform twenty feet in the air could be boring."

"Thank goodness I didn't disappoint you." But she got a glimpse of how his restless nature might feel confined in a typical relationship. He really wasn't suited for a cottage surrounded by a white picket fence.

"You couldn't if you tried. But I don't want you disappointing that professor who hired you, either. You need to get to work."

"I do."

"And if it's okay, I want to help. I love being your spotter."

"Then you're hired. How much do you charge?"

He laughed. "I've already been paid in full. This has been a great afternoon. Possibly the best of my life. Now let's get moving."

As they dressed and settled in to observe the eagle nest, she kept thinking about that comment. This had been a great afternoon for her, too. Possibly the best afternoon of her life. But she was reluctant to say so because she didn't want him to think she was getting attached.

He was free to say it, though, because he'd already declared his independence. He could rave about their time together, knowing that she wouldn't expect him to stay. It was a lopsided situation.

Somehow she'd set the record straight without being too obvious about it. She had to let him know in no uncertain terms that she didn't *want* him to stay. Then she could relax and make any appreciative remarks she cared to. She simply had to find the right moment.

LUKE HADN'T BEEN kidding. Today had been outstanding, an afternoon he wasn't likely to forget. He had high hopes for tonight, too. Sex in a tent could be a lot of fun. They'd also sleep in that tent, though. Both of them had to work the next day, and all he needed was for Emmett or Jack to catch him dragging around tomorrow.

As the sun started its descent, Luke announced his plan to cook dinner, and Naomi seemed grateful for that. He'd tucked two frozen steaks in his saddlebags, and they would be about ready to put on the grill now. He left her to finish up her work on the platform and walked back to the campsite.

Once there, he gathered firewood and soon had a nice little blaze going in the rock fire pit that he found near the tent. He took a couple of foil-wrapped potatoes and tossed them into the flames. The corncobs, still in their husks, would go on top of the grill once the flames died down a bit.

Next he fed Smudge oats, and because Luke still had a little time, he unrolled his sleeping bag in the tent. Hers was pushed over to one side. It might be the way she normally arranged it, but he'd pretend she'd done that to make room for him in case he showed up. He liked to think she'd hoped for that.

As he smoothed out the sleeping bag and tucked a couple of condoms under it, he found himself whistling. Good sex certainly could make a guy feel like a million bucks. And it wasn't only the good sex. Being with Naomi was a real kick.

He'd already started estimating how often he could make it out here. He wouldn't have another afternoon off for several days, but that didn't mean he couldn't spend some of his nights with her, if she didn't mind sharing her tent.

Normally when he became sexually involved with a woman, they got together only a couple of times a week. That had been plenty. He realized that his thinking was different this time, but he explained it away by the novelty of the situation.

His former girlfriends had lived in apartments, so they'd either spent time at his place or hers, or at a hotel for variety's sake. For some reason he'd never thought to take any of them camping. The professional women he'd dated hadn't seemed like the camping type. Maybe he hadn't given them enough credit, but he couldn't imagine any of them going without makeup and taking a quick bath in a mountain stream.

Today he'd learned something valuable about himself. He *loved* having outdoor sex during the day. He was amazed that he'd never tried it before, but now that he had, he was a real fan. Not every woman would agree with him on that, but he'd been lucky enough to hook up with a woman who was willing to go along.

Having a platform high in a tree helped, too. They weren't as likely to be caught in the act. Actually, if they were going to continue with those episodes, they'd be wise to bring the ladder up. That way they really couldn't be caught in the act. He'd see what Naomi thought about that suggestion.

Before he left the tent, he took off his hat and laid it brim-side up on what he now considered his side. A hat only got in the way when there was a beautiful

YOUR PARTICIPATION IS REQUESTED!

Dear Reader,

Since you are a lover of romance fiction – we would like to get to know you!

Inside you will find a short Reader's Survey. Sharing your answers with us will help our editorial staff understand who you are and what activities you enjoy.

To thank you for your participation, we would like to send you 2 books and 2 gifts – **ABSOLUTELY FREE!**

Enjoy your gifts with our appreciation,

Pam Powers

SEE INSIDE FOR READER'S SURVEY

YOUR READER'S SURVEY "THANK YOU" FREE GIFTS INCLUDE:

- 2 Harlequin® Blaze™ books
- 2 lovely surprise gifts

▶ DETACH AND MAIL CARD TODAY! ▶

PLEASE FILL IN THE CIRCLES COMPLETELY TO RESPOND

1) What type of fiction books do you enjoy reading? (Check all that apply)
❍ Suspense/Thrillers ❍ Action/Adventure ❍ Modern-day Romances
❍ Historical Romance ❍ Humour ❍ Paranormal Romance

2) What attracted you most to the last fiction book you purchased on impulse?
❍ The Title ❍ The Cover ❍ The Author ❍ The Story

3) What is usually the greatest influencer when you plan to buy a book?
❍ Advertising ❍ Referral ❍ Book Review

4) How often do you access the internet?
❍ Daily ❍ Weekly ❍ Monthly ❍ Rarely or never.

5) How many NEW paperback fiction novels have you purchased in the past 3 months?
❍ 0 - 2 ❍ 3 - 6 ❍ 7 or more

YES! I have completed the Reader's Survey. Please send me the 2 FREE books and 2 FREE gifts (gifts are worth about $10) for which I qualify. I understand that I am under no obligation to purchase any books, as explained on the back of this card.

150/350 HDL F5FN

FIRST NAME LAST NAME

ADDRESS

APT.# CITY

STATE/PROV. ZIP/POSTAL CODE

Offer limited to one per household and not applicable to series that subscriber is currently receiving.
Your Privacy—The Harlequin® Reader Service is committed to protecting your privacy. Our Privacy Policy is available online at www.ReaderService.com or upon request from the Harlequin Reader Service. We make a portion of our mailing list available to reputable third parties that offer products we believe may interest you. If you prefer that we not exchange your name with third parties, or if you wish to clarify or modify your communication preferences, please visit us at www.ReaderService.com/consumerschoice or write to us at Harlequin Reader Service Preference Service, P.O. Box 9062, Buffalo, NY 14269. Include your complete name and address.

HB-SUR-07/13

woman around, so why wear it? He wanted to be free to kiss her any old time he had a chance.

He had the corn and the steak cooking by the time she walked into camp. Even with her clothes and her hiking boots on, she still looked like a wood nymph. She matched the environment, and he liked that about her.

She sniffed appreciatively. "Smells wonderful, Luke. I haven't had steak in ages. You're hired as the camp cook, too."

"I'm happy to accept the job." He crouched down and turned the steak with the long-handled fork he'd brought with him. "I like to make myself useful."

He glanced over his shoulder and caught her eyeing his butt.

"You're *very* useful." She ogled him openly now, hamming it up. "There's something really sexy about a guy slaving over a hot campfire, especially when he can fill out a pair of jeans."

"Watch out." He grinned at her. "I'm liable to start feeling like a sex object."

"I know how you would hate that—having me pester you constantly to strip down so I can worship your body."

"Yeah, that sounds awful. When does the pestering start?"

"If that steak didn't smell like heaven, it would start right away. But I don't want to interfere with this promising meal preparation."

"Tactical mistake on my part." He stood. "I should

have waited to put on the steak until after you'd come back to camp, in case you wanted an appetizer."

"I'll settle for a kiss."

He laid the fork on a rock and walked toward her. "Think we can stop with a kiss?"

"With that steak sizzling on the grill? You bet. Every cowboy and cowgirl knows it's a crime to burn a good steak."

He cupped her face in both hands. "I'll keep that in mind." Then he tilted her head back and brushed the corner of her mouth with his thumb. "Open up, Naomi. I'm coming in."

She moaned softly and met him halfway, parting her lips and welcoming the thrust of his tongue. He delved into her warm mouth with the urgency of a man who'd been denied for weeks, instead of mere hours. She tasted so damned good.

Vaguely he heard a popping sound but didn't realize it was the sound of his shirt being unbuttoned until she slid both hands up his bare chest and pinched his nipples. His cock swelled in response. He lifted his mouth a fraction. "You're not playing fair."

"I didn't say I would."

"Then neither will I." He slipped a hand under the back of her T-shirt and unhooked her bra. Then when he made a frontal assault with that same hand, he discovered that her nipples were as rigid as his.

She moaned deep in her throat.

"You're asking for it," he murmured against her mouth.

"Uh-huh. Make it fast."

Fire licked through his veins. He backed her toward the tent. "Get in there and take off your shorts." He released her, unbuckled his belt and unfastened his jeans.

By the time he crawled in after her, she was in the process of kicking away her shorts and panties. He felt under his sleeping bag, located a condom and knelt at the tent entrance while he quickly took care of that chore.

Then he was on her. With his booted feet sticking out of the tent, he took her with such enthusiasm that he lifted her bottom right off the floor of the tent. She squeaked, but that squeak soon became a whimper as he pumped rapidly.

She came fast, and he followed right after. Then she started laughing, and he did, too. It was crazy to be doing this when it might mean ruining their meal.

But apparently she didn't plan for him to do that. "Go." She kept laughing as she gave him a little push. "Check the meat."

"What if I want some cuddling?"

"I'll cuddle you later! Don't burn the steak."

Grinning like a fool, he backed out of the tent, disposed of the condom and zipped up. He glanced over at the steak, which looked about perfect. Still chuckling, he made a megaphone of his hands. "Dinner's ready!"

God, but she was fun. Yep, best day ever.

9

"THIS STEAK is fabulous." Naomi sat on a flat rock with a tin plate balanced in her lap and a bottle of beer at her feet. Good sex followed by good food was a combination she hadn't had that often, but she'd like to make it a habit.

"I'll bet you say that to all your camp cooks." Luke sat cross-legged on the ground near her. The campsite had one decent sitting rock and he'd insisted she take it.

"I do. You're the first one I've ever had. Are you sure you're okay on the ground? I can go get the camp stool. I didn't even think about seating arrangements. I'm so used to eating alone here."

"Next time we can bring the stool down." He looked up from the ear of corn he was eating. "Assuming I'll get invited back."

"The odds of that are very good."

"I can bring you fresh food each time. I know you're surviving on energy drinks and canned goods, but that must get old."

"I consider it part of the job," she said. "The main focus is the eagles, and I just need to stay reasonably fed and hydrated so I'll be able to keep climbing that ladder."

"Which reminds me. Next time we decide to have sex up there, we—"

"Liked that, did you?" She was amused at his eagerness to continue their adventure. Amused and flattered. Something about this setup had touched a chord, and she wasn't going to argue about that. She reaped the benefits.

"I can't imagine why I've never had sex outside before. Maybe it was the fear of getting caught. That platform gives us a measure of privacy that's not easy to find."

She laughed. "I'm sure that's something Jack and Emmett didn't envision."

"They didn't count on me."

"Neither did I. But I'm so glad you showed up, Luke."

He held her gaze. "Me, too."

Maybe this was her perfect moment. "I've been thinking about something."

"So you had the same idea? Pull up the ladder so we don't get surprised by an unexpected visitor?"

"No, I didn't think of that, but it's a good idea. Yes, it will look suspicious, but better that someone imagines something is going on than that they see it in living color."

"My thought exactly."

"But that wasn't what I was going to say."

"Okay, shoot." He picked up his beer and took a swallow.

She loved looking at him sitting there, his shirt unsnapped at her request, his posture relaxed, happy. He was a gorgeous man. Even watching him drink his beer was a treat.

"What?" He smiled at her.

"You're incredibly good-looking, Luke."

He actually blushed. "That's not what you were going to say."

"No, but it doesn't hurt to tell you."

"You're not afraid it'll go to my head?"

"Actually, no. You're brash, but you're not conceited."

"Thank you." He put down his empty plate. "But you still haven't told me this big revelation."

"Okay. We had a discussion about my potential plans for the future. They're different from yours."

"Yes, they are."

"Just so you know, I realize the difference. When you said this was possibly your best afternoon ever, you could say it because you'd already announced your plans to leave. It was possibly my best afternoon ever, but I was afraid to say so, in case you'd think I was trying to, I don't know...trap you into something."

His expression brightened. "It was possibly your best afternoon ever?"

"Yes. But that doesn't mean that I—"

"I'm glad. I'm really glad. As for being worried that you'd try to trap me, I'm not."

"That's good, but why not? We get along and we

have great sex. Why wouldn't I want to try and change your mind?"

"Because you believe in the principle of live and let live. You're watching those eagles from afar. You're not trying to capture them and band them."

She nodded. Good observation on his part. "So if I'm enthusiastic about something we're doing together, you won't worry that I'm building castles in the air?"

"No. I trust you. If I didn't, I wouldn't be here."

"Fair enough."

"Ready for dessert?"

"You brought dessert?"

"Of course. Hang on." He stood and walked over to his saddlebags. He pulled out a plastic container. "I put them in here so they wouldn't get crushed."

Popping the top on the container, he showed her two chocolate cupcakes.

"Yum."

"Even better, they have cream filling."

"I love that." She reached for one.

"You know what I wish?" He took the other cupcake and returned to his spot on the ground.

"What?"

"That we didn't have to worry about bears. Because if we didn't have to worry about bears, we'd be eating these in the tent."

"You mean like at a slumber party?" She wasn't sure where he was going with this story.

"An X-rated slumber party. Yours would be served on my abs, and mine would be served in your cleavage."

"Mmm." She glanced over at him. "Hold that thought. You can bring cupcakes to the next picnic on the platform."

"Damn. I didn't think of that. We could have—"

"We don't have to do everything at once. I'll be out here until the nestlings fly." *And you leave.*

"You're right. Maybe we should pace ourselves. But you've given me a challenge. It'll be fun to think of all the interesting ways we can have sex between now and then."

"I'll look forward to your boundless creativity." She'd just had another insight. By setting a limit on their time together, he'd ramped up the tension. Lovers faced with a ticking clock always cherished the moments more than those who thought they had forever.

She needed to remember that truism as she joined him on this roller coaster. He was an exciting lover, but he was also a bit of an adrenaline junkie. He didn't know how to relax into a relationship and live it day by day. So she would accept him for the thrill ride that he was and understand that when the ride was over, he'd be gone.

LUKE WASN'T WORRIED that Naomi would let herself get attached to him, but it didn't hurt for her to say that she wouldn't. He let her go into the tent first and undress while he smothered the fire and made sure every trace of food was packed in airtight containers and stored in the sack she hung from a tree.

Someday he'd love to devour a cream-filled chocolate cupcake that was resting in the valley between her breasts, but he wasn't sure when that would be. Even if they met in town, she'd be staying with her parents. There would be no cupcake games under that roof.

But he wasn't about to complain. He stripped down outside the tent in deference to the cramped quarters. Then, holding the battery-operated lantern he'd used for the last stages of the cleanup operation, he crawled into the tent.

Entering a tent where a naked woman lay waiting was arousing enough. But when the light fell on her lounging like Cleopatra on her barge, he was immediately ready for action. His cock twitched with impatience as he zipped the tent closed.

He turned toward her and pretended shock. "My God! There's a stark-naked woman in this tent! What shall I do?"

She crooked a finger. "Come closer and let me whisper some suggestions in your ear."

"Excellent." He moved within range and set the lantern at the end of the tent before bending down to let her murmur sweet nothings. Except they weren't sweet. They were inventive and extremely specific. He proceeded to follow those suggestions, which involved Naomi rising to her hands and knees and Luke, once he'd rolled on a condom, taking her from behind.

Judging from her response, she liked that very much, so much that she climaxed in no time. He wasn't quite there yet, so he proposed the next phase, which involved lying on their sides facing each other with her leg hooked over his thigh. He stroked slowly as he caressed her warm breasts.

How he loved touching her. "I could do this all night."

"It wouldn't be a bad way to while away the hours."

"No, but let's take it up a notch." Reaching between her legs, he found her trigger point and began an easy massage as he continued to rock his hips back and forth.

She drew in a breath. "That's nice."

"I can tell." By the light of the lantern he could see her pupils dilate and her cherry-red lips part. His massage became more insistent. "Still nice?"

"You want me to come again."

"Bingo."

"I don't know if I…oh, Luke…*Luke*." She bucked against him, and that was all he needed. He climaxed with a grateful moan of release. Good. So good.

They lay there breathing hard, gazing at each other.

Reaching over, he stroked her mouth with his forefinger. "Thank you for today."

She sighed. "My pleasure." Her eyes drifted closed.

"Mine, too." He could tell she was tired and ready to sleep. He managed to ease out of her arms without disturbing her. Once he'd dealt with the condom, he switched off the light. "Good night, Naomi."

She was already asleep.

He lay in the dark listening to her breathe. In the distance an owl hooted. A small night creature scurried through the bushes somewhere near the tent. He felt at one with the night and the natural world. His heart filled with gratitude that she'd allowed him to share it with her.

He woke up to hear birds chirping and pale sunlight glowing on the sides of the tent. Naomi was gone. In a sudden panic, he sat up and grabbed his briefs and jeans.

Wherever she'd gone, she'd zipped the tent after leaving it. He took a deep breath. She'd probably left to go to the bathroom or put on coffee. Still, he had a strong urge to know where she was.

He crawled out of the tent wearing only his jeans and his briefs. He thought about pulling on his boots, but that would only slow him down. He needed to see her, needed to know she was okay.

She wasn't within sight. The campfire was still cold. He called her name softly in case she was nearby. No answer. Maybe this was why he'd never gone camping with a woman. You could lose track of them.

Maybe she'd gone to check on the eagles. The soles of his feet weren't used to pine needles and sharp rocks, and he winced as he made his way down the path to the platform. Climbing quickly, he stuck his head over the edge. Nope, not there.

Only one more place to look. He really should have put on his boots, but it was a little late to think about that now. He took the other trail, the one leading to the stream. The rocks seemed even sharper there.

Swearing under his breath, he gingerly picked his way along until he was in sight of the bubbling water. Then he sighed in relief. His wood nymph sat in the middle of the stream, up to her nipples in cold water.

He couldn't imagine how she could tolerate it, but she looked blissful with her hair slicked back and the water swirling around her. He started forward and stepped on a particularly sharp rock. He yelped and she turned to face him.

"Luke! What are you doing walking without your boots?"

"You did it." He saw no evidence of her clothes or her hiking boots on the shore.

"I'm used to being barefoot. Most cowboys aren't."

"That's a fact." But he was nearly there now. "How's the water?"

"Icy when you get in, but you get used to it."

"Really?" He had his doubts.

"After all that sex, I wanted a dip in the stream."

There was a gauntlet thrown down if he'd ever seen one. He'd had as much sex as Naomi, which meant he could use a dip in the stream, too. Or he could eat breakfast with her in his current unwashed state, which didn't seem particularly polite, now that he thought about it.

Hobbling to the edge of the stream, he unbuttoned his jeans and pulled down his fly. "I'm coming in."

"It'll feel really good once you adjust to the temperature."

He wished like hell he believed that. Vaguely he remembered that women had a different tolerance for heat and cold than men. It had to do with some primitive conditioning because they were the ones who had babies, so they needed protective fat layers. Something like that.

But he'd committed himself to this, and backing down would look bad. The very second he put his foot in the water, he regretted his decision. He deeply regretted it. Some people thought the Polar Bear Club was a great idea. He was not one of those people.

"Come on, Luke. Seriously, it feels great once you get past the first few steps."

Damn it. If he turned and went back, she'd think he was a wimp. But if he continued into that water, he might never be able to get it up again in this lifetime. His cock would freeze solid, which would do irreparable damage.

"You're not going to chicken out, are you?" Her laughter was the final straw.

"Absolutely not!" Gritting his teeth, he splashed toward her, and when he reached the spot where she sat chest-deep, he plopped right down. He thought he was going to have a heart attack. "Holy hell! This water's *freezing*." He would have stood up again, but he wasn't sure his legs would support him now that they were shaking like a willow branch in the wind.

"Wait it out. It gets better."

"No, it doesn't. You're numb by now. You're probably in shock. Can you feel your toes? I can't feel mine."

"You're such a baby. I do this every day."

His teeth started to chatter. "F-first thing in the m-morning?"

"Well, no. I usually wait until the middle of the day."

"Let's do that." He tried to get up, but the rocks were slippery and he was still pretty shaky. "Let's get out and try it again at noon."

She put a hand on his shoulder, so cold it felt like the clutch of death. "You won't be here at noon. Look, you're in the water now, so you might as well relax and enjoy it."

"You realize this could be the end of our sex life."

"How's that?"

"My cock is never going to be the same after this."

"Sure it will." She reached over and cupped his cheek. Her fingers were frigid. "Kiss me."

"The way my teeth are chattering, I might bite you instead."

"Try it."

He figured all was lost anyway, so he might as well go along with this kissing routine. Turning toward her, he tried not to quiver as their lips met. At first it was a chilly proposition, indeed, but then her warmth began to penetrate the frost.

The effect reminded him of a movie where the prince kissed the sleeping princess and she gradually turned from deathly white to pink and glowing. Only he was the deathly white prince and Naomi was the princess reviving him. The longer they kissed, the better he felt.

Soon he had so much feeling in his fingers that he remembered she was naked in this water and he could reach over and play with her breasts. So he did.

She drew away from his kiss. "See? You're starting to enjoy yourself."

"Some. Kiss me again."

"Sure." Sliding around to face him, she held his head and really began to kiss him with enthusiasm.

That helped enormously because now he could fondle both of her plump breasts at once, and as he toyed with her nipples, he felt the most incredible miracle happen. Even in water cold enough to chill a beer keg, his cock began to rise.

She nibbled on his lower lip. "I'm getting hot. How about you?"

"I wouldn't say I'm hot, but I'm hard."

"You are?" She reached under the water, swishing her hand around until she found him. "Oh, my goodness."

"They said it couldn't happen."

"Let's see what else might happen." She began to stroke him.

"Naomi, no." But he didn't pull away.

"Why not? Aren't men more potent in the morning? Let's take the edge off."

"I can't believe you're doing this." Still he didn't stop her. His balls tightened and his breathing grew shallow.

"You want me to. I can tell." Her tongue traced the curve of his lower lip as her hand moved faster. Then she caught his lip in her teeth and fondled the tip of his cock, squeezing, stroking....

He groaned. "Yes...ah...*yes*." He came, spurting into the cold water that no longer felt cold at all.

Her chuckle was rich with triumph. "Wasn't that great?"

He gasped, but not because he was cold. She'd taken care of that in fine fashion. "Great." He wondered if she was spoiling him for anyone else. Now, there was a truly scary thought.

10

Naomi had enjoyed her first week alone in the forest with the eagle family. But her second week had taught her more about herself than about the nesting habits of eagles. She'd spent her days studying and recording the raptors' behavior, but she'd spent her nights with Luke.

His arrival had depended on his duties. Sometimes he'd show up before sunset and they'd make love on her observation platform, surrounded by fiery hues and the twitter of birds settling in for the night. Other times he'd ride into her camp after dark, when she'd already built a fire in preparation for dinner.

On those nights, he'd swing down from the saddle and pull her into his arms with an impatient oath, as if he'd been gone for days instead of hours. The first time that had happened, he'd been so desperate that he'd backed her up against a tree. Thrilling though that encounter had been, she'd chosen to have a sleeping bag conveniently positioned by the fire the next time he'd arrived after dark.

Sharing her work space and her campsite with Luke was the closest she'd ever come to living with a man. Because she'd fared so well on her own, she'd always wondered how well she'd tolerate such an arrangement. She not only tolerated Luke's presence, she craved it.

With Luke she lost any lingering sexual inhibitions. Having sex with him every night had taught her how responsive she could be. She vowed not to lose that information after he was no longer inspiring her to enjoy her body to the fullest.

Luke had also raised the bar for any guy she would ever become involved with. Although she couldn't dream of a forever-after with Luke, she wouldn't settle for less than someone with his vibrancy. No more underdogs for her.

She was grateful that Luke Griffin had ridden under her tree nearly a week ago. As she swept the meadow with her binoculars around noon, she foolishly wished that he'd appear. He wouldn't, though, not for several hours.

She might have worried about her eagerness to see him, except that she could guarantee he was thinking of her at this very moment, too. Somehow he'd managed to perform his duties to Emmett's satisfaction, even though he'd told her that his thoughts were always on her. He'd described some of those thoughts, and they were all X-rated.

So were hers. Whenever she remembered all they'd shared this past week, she grew moist and achy. Sitting on the camp stool, she took off her hiking boots and socks, even though she knew for a fact he wouldn't be riding out into the clearing until the sun went down.

Standing barefoot on the platform, she still felt restricted by her clothing, so she stripped everything off. She'd love to walk around the platform naked, but after Jack's surprise visit, she wasn't comfortable doing that. She put her shorts and shirt back on, but going without underwear felt risky and fun. No doubt about it, Luke had changed her outlook.

Too bad he wouldn't be here for a sexy picnic. After checking the eagles and typing more notes, she snapped off a few shots with her digital camera. Then she grabbed an energy drink and paced the platform as she sipped it. She pictured what Luke might be doing right now.

He'd mentioned teaching roping tricks to the eight boys who were spending the summer at the ranch as part of Pete Beckett's youth program for troubled kids. Naomi smiled at the thought of Luke working with those boys. He had such an adventurous spirit that he probably had them eating out of his hand. He certainly had her eating out of it.

A movement on the far side of the clearing caught her attention. Quickly setting her energy drink on the folding table, she grabbed her binoculars and her pulse leaped. As if she'd willed him to be there, Luke was riding in her direction on Smudge. What a glorious sight.

Capping her energy drink, she gave in to what was probably a ridiculous impulse. She tugged on her hiking boots, leaving the socks off, climbed down the ladder and started across the meadow to meet him. He'd ridden this path so often that he'd worn a little trail she could follow through the ankle-high grass and wildflowers.

She knew the minute he'd spotted her, because he urged Smudge into a canter. Laughing, she started to run. She couldn't remember the last time she'd run without a bra, and her breasts jiggled under her shirt. This was crazy, but crazy was how he made her feel.

When they were about ten yards apart, she stopped running so she could catch her breath before they met. He slowed Smudge to a trot and then to a walk.

His grin lit up his entire face as he approached her. "I liked that."

"Which part?"

"You being so excited to see me that you had to race out here gave my ego a boost, and the fact that you're not wearing a bra made it even more fun to watch." He tipped back his hat with his thumb. "What's the occasion?"

"I felt like staying loose today."

"That sounds promising. Can I hope it was for my benefit?"

"Let's say it's for our benefit."

"Works for me." He drew alongside her. Sliding his booted foot out of the stirrup, he held out his hand. "Come on up."

"Is there room for me up there?"

"Plenty of room if you sit on my lap."

"Will Smudge be okay with that?"

"Smudge is so well trained you could do a lap dance and he wouldn't spook."

"Is that what you envision? Me doing a lap dance on horseback?"

"Nope. You don't have to do a thing except enjoy the ride." He wiggled his fingers. "Let's go."

She didn't need to be asked again. The sight of him cantering toward her, his body moving in rhythm with the horse, had aroused her beyond belief. She wanted to feel all that manly coordination up close and personal.

Placing her hand in his firm grip, she put her foot in the stirrup and swung up and over the horse's neck so she faced Luke. She marveled at the strength in his arm as he steadied her movements one-handed.

"Hold on to my shoulder."

He circled her waist with his free arm and cinched her in tight against his crotch. "There you go." He clucked his tongue and Smudge started walking down the trail. "How's that? Comfy?"

"You have no idea." She slipped her feet free of the stirrups and hooked her heels behind his knees so she could feel the hard ridge of his erection rocking against her as the horse moved. "I took off my panties, too."

He groaned. "You are rapidly becoming the sexiest woman I've ever had the good fortune to meet."

She wound her arms around his neck and lifted her face to his. "You've always been the sexiest man I've ever had the good fortune to meet."

"Then you won't be surprised if I put my hand up your shirt." He held the reins and focused on the trail ahead, but he slid his free hand under the hem of her shirt and cupped her breast. "I like this decision of yours to ditch the undies." Slowly he rolled her nipple between his thumb and forefinger. "I like it a lot."

Sensation zinged straight to the spot being massaged by the bulge in his jeans. "Mmm." She pressed against his fly and let the steady movement of the horse work its magic. "You can do that some more if you want."

He kept his attention on the trail. "You're trying to come, aren't you?"

"You told me to enjoy the ride."

He glanced down at her and his dark eyes glittered. "You realize what this means, right?"

"Yes." She sucked in a breath as she felt the first twinge. "I'm going to run out to meet you more often."

"It means that the minute we get off this horse, you and I will get very busy."

She moaned softly and rocked a little faster. "Doing what?"

"Take a guess. Now go for it, you loose woman." He pinched her nipple faster. "We're almost there."

"So am…I." When the spasms hit, she pressed her face against his shirt to muffle her cries. She didn't want to scare the horse. But, oh, this was fun. Before meeting Luke, she would never have dreamed of doing such a thing.

True to his word, Luke had her out of the saddle the minute they reached the shade of her pine tree. She was feeling pretty mellow, so she didn't mind when he laid her down on the pine-needle-and-leaf-strewn ground. His expression was so intense that she figured this would be an epic coupling.

He had her shorts off in a flash, but he wasted no time on his clothes. Hooking his hat on the saddle horn, he unbuckled his belt and wrenched down his zipper so he could free his cock and suit up. He didn't bother with foreplay, either. Moving over her, he spread her legs and drove in deep.

She expected him to pump fast and come quickly, but he surprised her. Once they were securely locked together, he propped himself up on his forearms and shifted so he could cradle her head in both hands. They stayed like that as he gazed down at her without moving. He seemed to be studying her.

Wrapping her arms around him, she looked into his eyes. They were still hot, but his expression had lost some of its desperation. "I thought you were in a hurry," she said.

"I was. To get here." Although he'd seemed to be up to the hilt, he managed to slide in a fraction more. "Right here."

"I thought I wouldn't see you until later."

"I switched afternoons with Shorty." He eased back and shoved home again. "I'll work for him tomorrow afternoon."

"Why?"

"I needed this." And he began a slow, steady rhythm as he held her gaze. "I needed…you."

The walls she'd carefully constructed around her heart began to weaken. He shouldn't say things like that. He didn't mean it the way another man might, but…how sweetly he was loving her. How easy to look into those warm brown eyes and imagine that something more than lust had captured him.

"I'm glad you're here." She grasped his hips and lifted to meet him. "I needed you, too."

He smiled as he continued the lazy back-and-forth movement. "Guess so. Running around the place without underwear. What were you thinking?"

"This."

"Yeah? You wanted to have sex on the ground?"

"No. I just…wanted you inside me."

"That's nice to hear, but how about a side order of a nice juicy orgasm?" He leaned down and brushed his mouth over hers. "I know you've already indulged, but…"

"I'll take another, please."

"I thought you might. FYI, don't yell. Smudge is a calm horse, but let's not push it."

"I won't yell."

"You might want to." Nibbling on her lower lip, he increased the pace slightly. "How's that feel?"

Tension coiled within her. "Good."

He moved a little bit faster. "And that?"

She gasped. "Better."

"Wrap your legs around me. We're going for best."

Once she did, opening to him completely, he took command, his rapid thrusts bringing her quickly to the edge and hurling her over.

As sensations brilliant as diamonds cascaded through her, she started to cry out. He kissed her hard, capturing her cries as he continued to pump again and again. At last, wrenching his mouth from hers, he groaned and plunged once more.

His body shook and he gulped for air. "Hope I didn't…hurt your mouth."

Her words were forced out as she panted. "No… sorry…forgot the horse."

"I'll take that…as a compliment."

"Do."

"Ah, Naomi." He leaned his forehead against hers. "You're every man's fantasy."

"I like the sound of that."

"And I like the feel of you…under me, on top of me, riding in front of me on my saddle while you give yourself a climax…." He lifted his head and smiled down at her. "You know what we should do now?"

"I can't imagine, but whatever it is, I'm up for it."

"See, that's what I'm talking about. You're ready for whatever."

"I am, if I can do it with you."

"Then let's go skinny-dipping in the stream. I'm all sweaty after that little episode. You, of course, are perfect and only a bit moist, but—"

"Liar. My hair's plastered to the back of my neck. But I thought you didn't like cold water."

"I think I'd like it better in the heat of the day than first thing in the morning."

She laughed. "Luke, it's still cold in that water, even at this time of day."

"Not as cold, I'll bet, and I want to prove to you I'm not a wuss. Also, I want to talk to you about something."

"What?"

"Nothing earthshaking, or at least I hope it's not, but I want your opinion. Let's go get in the water and talk. Unless you need to check on the eagles."

"The webcam's babysitting the eagles and I changed the batteries this morning. We can skinny-dip."

"Great."

Twenty minutes later, Luke had staked Smudge to his grazing spot and they stood by the stream like Adam and Eve. Their clothes lay on the bank, along with Naomi's beach towel.

"I'm going first." Luke started down to the water. "To prove I'm a manly man."

"You don't have to prove that to me, cowboy." She drank in the sight of his tight buns, muscled back and strong thighs. Talk about a fantasy.

He stepped into the water and his breath hissed out.

"Want to change your mind?" Naomi couldn't help smiling. He was a baby about cold water. "We could put some water in a saucepan and let it warm in the sun. Then you could take a sponge bath."

"Nope. I'm doing this." Taking a deep breath, he plunged in, sending water splashing as he plowed over to the deepest part, which was still less than three feet. Then he sat down with another loud splash and a strangled groan.

"That was quite a production."

"It's cold as hell."

"I told you."

"Shouldn't it be warmer by now?"

"Did you happen to notice there's still snow on the mountains?"

"Yeah."

"That's where this water comes from. It's snow-melt."

"Oh." He glanced over at her. "You're coming in, right?"

"Of course. I do this every day." She stepped into the water.

"How come you're not shivering?"

"I have this mental trick. As I'm immersing myself in cold water, I visualize it being warm." She made her way over to him and sat down.

"You can do that?"

"Sure. So could you. Don't think about the water as being cold. Tell yourself it's like bathwater."

He gazed at her. "I'm going to visualize having sex with you, instead. That should heat me up really fast."

"If you keep looking at me like that, you'll heat me up, too. And then what?"

His slow smile hinted at watery pleasures. "We'll do something about it."

Despite what they'd already shared today, her body responded. "I thought you wanted to talk. But if you'd rather get friendly instead, you're headed in the right direction."

He sighed. "Right. I do want to talk. It's just that you're so beautiful. I can't seem to get enough of you."

"Then talk fast."

He chuckled. "Okay. It's about my dad."

11

"YOUR DAD?" Naomi stared at him, clearly startled.

He should have led up to it more gradually, but they'd become so close in the past week that he'd forgotten she didn't know anything about his parents. Yet why would she? He'd never told her. But now he needed a friend's advice. He would have gone to Nash, except Nash was involved in wedding and honeymoon plans. And besides, this was the sort of touchy-feely situation that he sensed Naomi would understand. He trusted her.

"Let me back up." He gazed down at the water and trailed his fingers through it. "It's been easier to focus on the fun you and I are having. I'm not into deep analysis of my past anyway."

"So what about your dad?"

Luke looked out across the water tumbling over rocks and gathered his thoughts. "He always claimed he wanted to travel and see the world, but because he married my mother, who hates travel, and he has the responsibilities of a home and his job, he's never gone anywhere."

"That's too bad."

He took a deep breath. "I talked to Emmett about it last week, and he started me thinking. My dad could travel, if he'd allow himself to. If my mom doesn't want to go, that's up to her. But I'm considering calling him and asking him to come out here, maybe even for the Fourth of July. He'd have a little time off then."

Luke had never done anything like this before, and he was surprised he hadn't. Maybe all that his dad needed was someone to say, "Hey, come on, let's go." On the other hand, if Luke invited him and he refused, that rejection would be tough to take. It might also mean his dad's spirit was truly crushed, assuming he'd ever really had a vagabond spirit in the first place.

"I think that sounds wonderful, Luke."

He looked over at her, drawing strength from the certainty in her blue eyes. "So I should do it?"

"Definitely. Where do your parents live?"

"New Jersey. He'd have to fly out, but he could. They have money. Hell, I'd pay for his flight if necessary."

She opened her mouth. Closed it again.

"If you have advice, please give it. That's why I asked you about this before I did anything. I want to make sure I'm not crazy to consider it."

"Okay. I wonder…maybe it would be better if you let him pay."

"You think so?" Luke thought about his mother,

who could raise an objection about the cost of a plane ticket, especially at the last minute.

"It would mean he's making more of a commitment to traveling, which you said he's always wanted to do."

Luke nodded. "You're right. But it could be pricey."

"It probably will be. But if he's been saying all his life that he wants to travel and he never has, then he's saved a lot of money by not traveling."

"That's a good point."

"The biggest thing is whether he can move that fast, but maybe choosing a last-minute vacation is better. Still, this is… My gosh, it's July 1 already, Luke. You should call him right away."

He knew that, too, and he'd wanted her support while he did that, but her location didn't help matters. "I don't know if my cell phone will work out here. It's an older one. Sometimes it gets a signal in this area and sometimes it doesn't."

"Did you bring it?"

"Yes." That was a huge admission because he never brought his phone, first of all because his reception was dicey and second of all because he didn't want to be interrupted when he was with her.

She stood. "We need to go back to camp so you can try to call."

He gave her a rueful smile. "You're right, but we just got here. I'm not sure we've dipped enough skinny."

That made her laugh. He loved it when she laughed, because she seemed to glow with happiness.

"The stream's not going anywhere," she said. "We'll have more chances. The phone call can't be postponed."

No, it couldn't, unless he abandoned the idea. But now that the concept had penetrated his thick skull, he wanted to act on it, especially if Naomi thought he should. He put a lot of faith in her opinion.

So they took turns using her beach towel to dry off. She dressed more quickly than he did now that she'd decided to dispense with underwear. He got such a kick out of that. She was turning out to be quite a seductive woman.

He figured that their week together had something to do with that. Oh, hell, *he* had something to do with that. Might as well admit that he'd coaxed her into becoming less inhibited.

And now what, genius? Will you go off and leave her, so that some other yahoo can reap the rewards? Or does that stick in your craw a little bit?

It did. But unless he planned to stay in Shoshone and make things permanent between them, which he didn't, then he had to live with the fact that she'd bestow her newly discovered sexuality on some other lucky slob. Better not to think about that.

Back in camp, wearing his jeans and boots with his shirt left unbuttoned, he pulled his cell phone out of his saddlebag and turned it on. As he'd feared, the signal was weak. It would be better in town or back at the ranch, but he didn't want to leave Naomi so he could make a damned phone call.

He turned his phone around to show her the bars, or lack of them. "I can call tomorrow."

"Or you can ride back."

"No." He didn't like that scenario at all. He'd always

been able to slip away from the ranch without attracting any notice, but if he went back to make a phone call, someone would see him, and leaving again would be problematic.

Besides, he wanted Naomi's moral support, and he couldn't very well take her back with him. If he had to call tomorrow without her, so be it, but he wasn't leaving her tonight to make that call, no matter what she said.

She slapped her forehead. "Luke, we should try your phone from the observation platform. That might make all the difference. The signal is stronger for my laptop, so it should be stronger for your phone, too."

"Sure, okay. We can climb up there. Let me get the cold fried chicken I brought."

"You brought *chicken?* Why haven't I heard about this before?"

"Sorry. I've been a little preoccupied."

"No kidding. I *love* fried chicken. If I'd known that you brought some, I would have—"

"Wanted that instead of sex? Then I'm glad I didn't mention it." He crouched down and pulled the plastic container out of his saddlebag. "Remind me never to make you choose between sex with me and fried chicken."

She gave him a saucy smile. "Why can't I have both?"

"Oh, you can. I'm just worried about how you order your priorities. I want to be at the top, but I have a feeling that when it comes to fried chicken, I'm not.

And I—oof!" He nearly fell over as she launched herself at him.

"Listen here, my friend." She wound her arms around his neck. "I don't know how many times I have to say this before it makes an impression, but sex with you is the best thing that's ever happened to me in my entire life. Yes, I love fried chicken. And beautiful sunsets and baby eagles and the sound of the wind through the pines. But I would forgo them all for an hour alone with a naked Luke Griffin."

He couldn't have wiped the grin off his face if someone had offered him a million dollars to do it. She'd laid it on pretty thick and he wasn't sure he could believe all of it, but he appreciated the effort more than she'd ever know.

He cleared his throat. "Thank you. I'll probably still be thinking about that speech when I'm a white-haired old geezer who can't get it up anymore."

"You actually think the day will come when you can't get it up anymore?"

He laughed. "No, I don't, but that sounded good, didn't it?"

"It sounded like you're still fishing for compliments about your awesome package." She patted his cheeks. "Bring your chicken and your cell phone and your package up to the platform, okay?"

"Yes, ma'am." Luke followed her down the path to the pine tree that supported her observation platform. He knew she'd been teasing him and acting sexy on purpose to take his mind off the impending conversation, assuming he could make the phone call from her platform.

That was exactly why he'd sought her out once he'd dreamed up this plan. She was the soft landing spot if he should fall and go splat, psychologically speaking. He stood below the ladder and concentrated on the pleasure of watching her climb it. By tilting his head, he could almost see up her shorts. Not quite, but he knew she wasn't wearing anything underneath and that was enough to fuel his imagination.

He wasn't sure if he wanted this phone call to go through or not. He had such mixed emotions about it. But at least, whatever happened, Naomi would be there at the end of it. And he could lose himself in her lush body...if she wasn't too absorbed with eating fried chicken.

NAOMI HAD SENSED all along that Luke's wandering soul had a soft, vulnerable spot somewhere within it. Maybe she'd been afraid to find out what that was because she already cared too much for the guy. Discovering his secret pain could tear down the walls around her heart completely, and those walls were already displaying stress fractures.

But he'd come to her, like a bird with a broken wing, and asked for help. She could no more deny that than she could toss an injured animal out into the elements. Her creed was to live and let live, but when that life hung in the balance, was she supposed to turn away?

She was no psychologist but even she could figure out that Luke had become a wanderer partly by nature but largely so that he could live the life his father had said he wanted. Maybe he'd hoped to please his father and maybe he'd wanted to compete. It didn't matter. He'd come to a crossroads, a place where he wanted to invite his father to share in his adventures.

Luke knew his dad's response to the invitation was important to both father and son. She didn't have to tell him that. Whether it was important to her was another question.

She could no longer deny that she was getting emotionally involved with this drifter who had wandered under her observation platform one bright, sunny day. She knew how much he'd come to mean in her life. She was less convinced how much she meant to him.

Yes, he needed her now, when he was about to make this difficult phone call to his father. But was she only a temporary crutch to get him through this critical time in his life? Or had they made a deeper connection?

She had no answers. But while he stood at a far corner of the deck and dialed the number for his parents' home, she laid out their picnic on the red checkered cloth he'd left there after their first meal on this platform. Regardless of how the call went, she would offer him solace.

If that cost her dearly in the long run because she ended up with a broken heart, she'd deal with that. He'd given her so much in this past week that she couldn't begrudge him whatever he needed. She mentally crossed her fingers and hoped that his father would understand the stakes when he heard Luke's invitation.

She didn't eavesdrop, but she knew when he'd made

a connection because the low murmur of his voice drifted over to her. Sitting beside the picnic tablecloth, she stayed very still, not wanting to disrupt his concentration in any way. This could be one of the most important conversations he'd ever have with his dad.

After what seemed like an eternity but was probably less than five minutes, Luke walked over and sat cross-legged on the far side of the checkered tablecloth. Glancing over at her, he shrugged. "He says he'll think about it and get back to me."

She wanted to scream. Stupid, stupid father! She tried to imagine her own father acting with such indifference. He never would. She thought of the Chance men, devoted fathers, every one of them.

She'd been in Florida when Jonathan Chance had died in a truck rollover, and she'd heard the rumor that he'd been upset with his son Jack at the time. Yes, that had been difficult for Jack to reconcile. But at least Jonathan had been a big part of Jack's life.

All of Jonathan's sons—Jack, Nick and Gabe—were passionately involved with their children. Nick wasn't biologically connected to Lester, the troubled boy he and Dominique had adopted after Lester had spent last summer at the ranch. But Nick was a committed parent.

Naomi searched for the right thing to say. "I'm sure you caught him by surprise. It's hard to make snap decisions."

His dark eyes were bleak. "No, it's not. You and I make them all the time. It's what you do when you're actually living life, instead of hanging on the fringes of it." Anger and disappointment rolled off him in waves.

"Don't give up."

"I won't. But the only way I'll get his call is if I'm up here."

"Then we'll stay up here."

He held her gaze. "Thank you. I…" He looked away and swallowed.

That's when she knew that he needed something more than fried chicken right now. Moving purposefully, she cleared all the food aside. He watched her without moving.

Then she sat on the tablecloth, right in front of him. Cupping his face in both hands, she kissed him as thoroughly as she knew how, putting all her caring, her longing and her passion into that kiss. At first he simply let her kiss him without responding.

That was a new experience for her, and one she didn't care for in the least. Luke had always been eager for her kisses. Once their lips met, he'd usually been the one who had pushed the kiss to the next level.

Not now, and for a brief moment her courage failed her. But she'd told him not to give up, and so she couldn't, either. She kissed his forehead, his eyes, his cheeks and once again his mouth.

With that the floodgates opened. With a groan, he pulled her into his lap. After that she didn't have to worry about how to kiss him. He took care of all the mouth-to-mouth contact, and the mouth-to-body contact, and every form of contact that followed.

Soon she lay sprawled naked on the tablecloth, and he'd covered every inch of her with his mouth and tongue. If she had been an ice-cream cone, she'd be long gone by now.

Standing, he gazed down at her as he took off his clothes with deliberate intent. "I'm going to have you six ways to Sunday," he said. "And then we'll start over and go through the whole damn week again."

"Okay." She watched him pull off his boots with angry motions and shuck his jeans and briefs. But after he'd located the condom in his pocket and put it on, she sat up and reached for his hand. "Lie down here. Lie down and let me love you for a change."

The fierceness left his expression as if a cloud had scudded away from the sun. Without a word, he knelt down and stretched out on the tablecloth. Her heart constricted with the surrender implicit in his reaction. This was what he wanted, what he needed—not to take her six ways to Sunday, but to be loved and cherished by someone who asked nothing in return.

What an easy assignment that was. Straddling him, she began with his beautiful face. She followed the curve of his cheekbones with her tongue and placed butterfly kisses on his eyelids. His mouth became a playground for her lips, his determined jaw a place to nibble and tease until she felt him slowly relax.

With a deep sigh he let his arms fall to his sides, and she traced each vein, each corded muscle in those arms with her fingertips. As his mighty chest rose and fell with his labored breaths, she toyed with his nipples and stroked the silky black hair covering that massive display of strength and power.

She followed the trail of dark hair to his navel, and

as she dipped her tongue into the shallow depression, he quivered. She stroked his cock and wished that nothing prevented her from feeling the velvet-on-steel wonder of it. But she could also fondle what lay beneath and watch as those heavy sacs drew up in tight readiness.

"Take me," he murmured. "Please take me."

She wondered if he'd ever begged a woman in his life. Maybe not. But she wouldn't make him do it more than once. Rising above him, she guided his taut cock into position and began a slow slide downward.

His breathing quickened as she descended, and when she'd taken all of him, he began to tremble. "Go slow," he said. "I don't want to come yet."

Leaning forward, she feathered a kiss over his lips and felt him sigh. Then she lifted her head to look into his eyes. "Tell me," she said softly. "Tell me what you need."

Passion burned in his gaze. His hands found her hips, bracketing them. "Easy strokes." His voice was strained. "Go easy. Let me… I want to wait."

She lifted up only a little and made her way gradually back down.

"Good." He held her gaze. "Again."

She repeated the motion.

He groaned. "So good. Again."

Once more she rose up and came slowly down.

He sucked in a breath. "Good Lord, I want you, Naomi. I want to come. But I don't want to end this."

She smiled. "We can do it again sometime."

A fire ignited in his eyes. He swallowed. "Then ride

me, lady." His words echoed their first time together. His fingers gripped her hips. "Ride me hard."

That was all she'd been waiting for. Yes, he needed the sweet loving, but more than that, he needed heat that would burn away grief, incinerate sadness. She brought the heat, pumping up and down with a frenzy that made her breasts dance and her bottom slap against his thighs.

His first cry was low and intense, his second louder and when he came, his shout of triumph sent the songbirds fluttering and squawking from the branches of the tree. He laughed at that, a breathless, happy sound that resonated in her heart.

She laughed with him, collapsing against his chest and panting from the effort she'd made.

He wrapped her tight in his arms. "Thank you, thank you, thank you. I know you didn't come."

"It doesn't matter."

"It does. I'll make it up to you." He rocked her in his arms. "I will make it up to you a dozen times over. But that…Naomi…that was exactly what I needed."

"I know."

"How did you know?"

"That's my secret." And it would remain her secret. If he ever guessed she was falling in love with him, he'd leave.

12

LUKE WASN'T SURE what he'd done to deserve someone like Naomi, but she was a lifesaver. As the sun went down, she insisted they should haul the sleeping bags up to the platform for the night. Even when he protested that his father was probably in bed by now and wouldn't call, she refused to consider going back down to the campsite, where the phone reception was bad.

"Just don't let me fall off in the middle of the night," she said, laughing.

The thought made his heart stutter and he stopped unrolling the sleeping bags. "Do you think you might? Are you a sleepwalker?"

"No. At least I don't think so."

"Let's forget this." He started bundling up his sleeping bag. "If there's the slightest chance that you'll wake up at night and start wandering around this platform half-asleep, it's not worth the risk."

"I won't. And we're staying." She crossed her arms and planted her feet. "I've always thought it would be fun to sleep up here, but I was a little worried about doing it by myself. This is perfect." She peered at him. "Unless *you're* a sleepwalker."

"Nope. Never been a problem for me." He crouched next to his sleeping bag, thinking. "So spending the night up here would be an adventure for you?"

"Yes. Absolutely."

"You're not just saying that because of the phone thing?"

"That's a good excuse to do it, but from the moment I first climbed onto the platform, I thought of spending the night, pretending I'm Tarzan. I've just been too chicken."

He smiled. "You wouldn't make a very good Tarzan."

"You'd be surprised." She took a deep breath and let out the most Tarzan-like yell he'd ever heard.

He laughed so hard he had to sit down.

"Wait, that wasn't as good as I can do. I'll try again." She sucked in more air.

"No, no, you're great!"

She looked at him. "Yeah?"

"Amazingly good. I wasn't laughing because you were lousy at it. I was laughing at that big Tarzan yell coming out of such a blonde cutie-pie. It's so unexpected."

"My college friends and I taught ourselves to do it. When we backpacked through Europe, we sometimes entertained people in pubs by doing our Tarzan yells. I'm better after a couple of beers."

"I'll bet." He chuckled. "I can just imagine that." He

also felt a pang of longing. Although he'd traveled with friends when he was younger, they'd all settled down with families. They still traveled, but now it involved taking spouses and kids, which was a whole other ball game. Not his deal.

He stood and surveyed the platform. "So if this is something you want to do for the adventure factor, but you're a little scared of falling off, we'll put your sleeping bag next to the tree and mine next to yours so I'm on the outside."

She nodded. "I like that. Thanks."

"You're welcome. It'll be fun." He knew that for sure because everything involving Naomi was fun. He couldn't remember the last time he'd laughed this much.

They ate cold sandwiches for dinner, watched a family of deer graze in the clearing and made love to the sound of wind in the trees. They slept spoon-fashion, with Luke on the outside. He figured if he kept a hand on her at all times, she wouldn't get away from him and risk falling.

That thought made him restless. And then there was the issue of a potential phone call. It didn't come until dawn, and it woke them both.

Luke scrambled to pick it up before the chime disturbed Naomi, but he was too late. She sat up, rubbing her eyes, as he put the phone to his ear.

"Luke, it's Dad."

Luke grimaced. "Hi, Dad." Who else would it be at this hour of the morning? His father had probably forgotten the time difference. Travelers usually thought about that when they made phone calls. Nontravelers, not so much.

"Listen, I thought about your invitation, and it won't work for me."

Luke had prepared himself for that answer, but even so, disappointment sliced through him. Apparently he'd placed more importance on this than he should have. "Okay."

"I checked flights, and it'll cost an arm and a leg."

"So it's the money?"

"Well, that, and your mother has a cookout planned with the Sullivans. She has her heart set on that cook-out. You remember the Sullivans, don't you?"

"Yep." They were neighbors whose attitude toward travel was exactly like his mother's. They claimed everything they needed was right there, so why go anywhere else?

"Anyway, thanks for asking. Maybe next time."

"Sure, Dad. Have a nice Fourth. Talk to you later." Luke disconnected and laid down the phone.

"He's not coming."

Naomi put a hand on his shoulder. "Luke, I'm sorry. It was a great idea."

He shrugged. "I should have known better. He'll just keep watching documentaries about places he'll never see."

"His loss."

"I think so, too, but I can't make him get out there and see the world." He gazed at her. "I did think it would be cool, though. I've never been here for Fourth of July, but the town's really gearing up. Are you coming in or staying here?"

She smiled. "Are you inviting me to come and party with you?"

"Hell, yes! We'll have a blast. Although maybe the fireworks will look more spectacular from this platform, come to think of it. We could—"

"Hold on. Did you say *fireworks?*"

"Yeah. Everyone's all excited because Shoshone's never had fireworks before. What's the matter? Don't you like fireworks?"

"That depends. Are we talking about little stuff, close to the ground? Backyard fireworks?"

"Not from what I heard. This Clifford Mason guy, the one we saw having dinner with Pam Mulholland at the Spirits and Spurs, is arranging for a huge spectacular. Tyler Keller…you know Tyler?"

"Yes, she's Josie Chance's sister-in-law. She plans tourist-type events for the town. So she set this up?"

"I believe that's what Emmett said. And Pam's underwriting it. Everybody's happy about it except Emmett, who thinks Clifford's romancing Pam."

"Luke, this is a disaster. I have to stop it."

"I don't think it's our place to interfere in Pam's private life."

"Not that. The fireworks. I know people will be disappointed and I hate that, but we can't have fireworks."

"Why not?"

She gestured toward the eagles' nest. "It's too close. The parents might become terrified and abandon the nest. The babies would die."

"Town's not *that* close."

"I know it doesn't seem like it, because from the ranch road it's about ten miles. But we're out on a far corner of Last Chance land. When I hike in from my folks' place, it's only about five miles straight across. That's way too close to nesting eagles."

He sensed a train wreck coming. "Are you sure the eagles would abandon the nest?"

"Not a hundred percent sure. You can't ever be positive when you're trying to predict the behavior of wild creatures. But I'm sure enough that I don't want to take the risk."

"Okay, but I'm afraid you're going to have some tough sledding. Everyone in town is looking forward to this."

"I'm sure they are. If it weren't for the eagles, *I* would be looking forward to it. But we do have eagles, and fireworks are a bad idea. Tyler's a very compassionate person. When I explain the situation, I'm sure she'll cancel."

He wasn't so sure. "I don't want to be the prophet of doom, but there could be economic repercussions. The fireworks have been paid for and the merchants are expecting to cash in on all the excitement."

"But what about the other activities? They always have a ton of things going on. Won't that be enough?"

"I don't know. Maybe, maybe not. I think you'll get push back. That's all I'm saying."

"I know." Her blue eyes clouded with sadness. "I really hate that, and I hate having people disappointed.

But I can't let them light up the sky only five miles from a nest of eagles."

"No, you can't. I can see that." He picked up his phone and hit a speed-dial number.

"Who are you calling?"

"Reinforcements." He gave her a quick grin. "Hello, Emmett? Listen, I need to take the morning off, if there's any way you can arrange it."

"I probably can," Emmett said. "What's the problem?"

"You might want to take the morning off, too. Naomi needs to shut down the fireworks display and she could use backup. Fireworks are a danger to the eagles. The parents might spook and abandon the nest."

"Is that so?" Emmett sounded pleased. "Never did care much for fireworks, myself."

"Or the guy who sells them?"

"Don't much care for him, either."

"I was thinking we need to have a little chat with the folks involved, but I don't have everybody's numbers."

"I can arrange a meeting," Emmett said. "How soon can you both get to the diner?"

"Thirty minutes to get organized and an hour of travel time, maybe less if Smudge is feeling lively this morning."

"Good. I'll round up the parties involved and meet you both at the diner in an hour and a half."

"Sounds good."

"Thanks for the call, Luke. It made my day."

"I thought it might. See you soon, Emmett." Luke

disconnected the phone and glanced over at Naomi. "Does that work for you?"

Grabbing his face in both hands, she kissed him soundly before releasing him. "Yes, sir, it most certainly does."

RIDING DOUBLE ON a five-mile trip turned out to be an interesting experience. Neither of them thought it would be wise to try it with Naomi sitting on Luke's lap facing him. They couldn't handle the distraction.

So they chose for Luke to sit forward in the saddle, with Naomi perched behind him, hanging on to his waist. Once they were settled, she couldn't see where they were going, but she trusted Luke to get them there safely.

She was, however, concerned about his package. "Are you squished up there?"

He chuckled. "A little. Can't be helped."

"I don't want you to injure yourself."

"I'll be fine unless the conversation turns to sex. Any expansion could jeopardize this entire arrangement."

"Understood. Maybe we shouldn't talk at all."

"We should definitely talk. If we ride along in silence, with your luscious body pressed tight against mine, my imagination will get me into trouble in no time. So think of a topic. Just don't make it anything sexy."

"I know the perfect thing. Tell me about some of your favorite places."

"Well, your mouth, and your—"

"No! In the world!"

"Oh." He laughed. "My mistake."

"You knew what I meant."

"Yeah, I knew what you meant. But sometime, not now, I'll list my favorite places on Naomi Perkins."

"You're not helping your cause, Luke."

"You're right. Okay, favorite places in the world. Jackson Hole is one of them, believe it or not."

"I believe it." She rested her cheek against his broad back. "I've always felt lucky that my parents chose to live here. So, what else?"

He began to list the places he'd seen that had made the biggest impression on him. He'd traveled widely in the United States and had made it to several South American countries. He'd also seen most of Australia and New Zealand. He talked lovingly about his trips, leaving no doubt that being a wanderer was in his blood. It was a good thing he knew that about himself.

About halfway there, he switched the conversation to her and she listed all her favorite spots, although she didn't have nearly as many as Luke. Privately she admitted that his life had some appeal, but she still thought it sounded like a lonely existence.

Thanks to their conversation, the trip went by faster than she'd expected. She didn't stop to think about the message she and Luke would convey with this cozy riding position until they were almost there.

She'd enjoyed resting her cheek on his warm, strong back, but she'd be wise to stop doing that. "I wonder if I should get off here and walk in."

"Why would you—? Oh, I get it. Wagging tongues.

Do you want to walk in? You're the local girl, so you decide. I told Emmett that we'd ride in together, but he probably won't mention it to anyone."

"He won't have to. If we ride down Main Street like this, I can guarantee we'll be noticed. Comments will be made. I may be the local girl, but you'll probably be hit with some personal questions. Assumptions will be made."

"I figure that'll happen anyway if we spend Fourth of July in town together, so I'm okay with it. Your call, though."

She thought about how he'd jumped right in on her side of the argument regarding the eagles. He'd pulled Emmett in, too, which was a brilliant move and something she might not have thought of.

She hadn't been privy to the semicourtship between Emmett and Pam Mulholland, but Luke, having worked at the ranch for nearly a year, knew all about it. Emmett Sterling was respected in Shoshone. If he supported the eagles, that would go a long way toward helping their cause.

"You know what, Luke? If you don't mind having people assume we're a couple, I don't mind, either."

"Good. That makes life less complicated in some ways. But by saying *people,* are you including your parents?"

"Um..." Their opinion wasn't as easy to ignore as everyone else's. She hesitated.

"You're not so sure about them, are you?"

"No."

"Is your father a shotgun-totin' man?"

That made her laugh. "He owns guns, if that's what you're asking. Most people around here do."

"Yes, but would he use a gun to make sure a fellow did right by his daughter?"

"No, he wouldn't. That's an old-fashioned view and I can't believe he'd ever take that kind of stand. Besides, I'm an adult, and I've been on my own for quite a while. But I'd hate for either my mom or my dad to think poorly of you."

"So?"

"So I'll talk to them and explain the situation." She didn't look forward to that, because her parents were eager for her to find the right guy. If she seemed interested in Luke, they would be, too—as a potential son-in-law. She had to nip that concept in the bud.

"Do you want me there for that conversation?"

"Good heavens, no." But she appreciated the courage it took for him to make the offer. "Thanks for your willingness, but I'll handle it."

As they rode down the street toward her parents' diner, she noticed the festive bunting decorating each storefront. Most shops also proudly displayed a poster advertising Shoshone's Fourth of July celebration and the word *fireworks* took center stage on the poster. She felt a little like the Grinch.

But two vulnerable young eagles might die as a result of those fireworks, and she couldn't believe her friends and family would want those nestlings to pay the price for a human celebration they couldn't escape. If she'd known about this sooner, she might have avoided a confrontation two days before the scheduled event.

She searched her memory. Had the information been out there and she'd simply missed it? Maybe. For the past month she'd been totally engrossed in the eagles, and more recently she'd been focused on Luke, as well. She hadn't needed to make trips to town, because he'd come out every night laden with food. One midweek trip would have told her what was coming down the pike.

When she had hiked in more than a week ago, no one had thought to inform her of the big plans because she hadn't been involved with them. She'd been gone for so many years, first for college and later for her job in Florida. She wasn't hooked into the rumor mill anymore. After this episode, she'd be *fodder* for the rumor mill.

A few businesses in Shoshone still had hitching posts in front of them, and the Shoshone Diner was one of those. It was at the far end of the curbside parking.

Logistics required Naomi to dismount first.

As Luke swung down to stand beside her, he chuckled. "One disadvantage to riding double is that I couldn't help you down from the saddle like a true gentleman."

"People understand that."

"I hope so, because I'm already going to be in trouble with your folks. I don't want them to add a lack of manners to my other sins."

"I won't let them blame you for anything."

He smiled. "Good luck. I expect they'll blame me

for everything. But don't worry. I can take it." Then he tied Smudge to the rail.

She supposed that he could take it. For his sake, that was a good thing. But in some ways, she wished that someone would finally pierce his coat of armor and touch the man underneath.

13

Before they walked into the diner, Luke took Naomi's laptop out of the saddlebag and handed it to her. "Ready?"

"I am. I wish I'd had time to get some of the pictures printed to pass around, but at least we have something to show."

He took her by the shoulders. "You'll do great." Then he gave her a quick kiss, because the way he saw it, he'd already been labeled as her boyfriend. Might as well take advantage of that label.

"Thanks, Luke." She smiled. "I'm glad you're here."

"Wouldn't miss it." He walked to the door and held it open for her. When they stepped into the crowded diner, all conversation stopped. Luke had never been in that situation before. Unfortunately the belligerent stares from people seated at the various tables eating breakfast weren't directed at him. He would have preferred that, but all the glares were focused on Naomi.

He gave her shoulder a squeeze before they started

over to the spot where two tables had been pushed together. Obviously this was the setting for the powwow. Emmett was already there, sitting on the far side on Pam Mulholland's right, and the dandified cowboy Clifford Mason had positioned himself on her left. Tyler Keller, a dark Italian beauty, had taken the opposite side of the table, flanked by Nick and Jack Chance.

Luke wasn't sure why the Chance boys had come, but then he remembered Nick was Pam's nephew. He might have come to give his aunt some moral support. As for Jack…well, Jack didn't like to miss out on anything. The mood at the table was decidedly tense.

A red-haired waitress bustled around the table filling coffee mugs, but nobody had food yet. Edgar Perkins, a tall man who wore glasses and was going bald, stood talking to Jack. His wife, Madge, wasn't in evidence.

Then she came out of the kitchen. A trim blonde with her hair in a ponytail and an apron tied over her jeans and Western shirt, she looked like Naomi probably would in twenty-five years. She walked straight over to her daughter and gave her a hug. "Whatever support you need from us," she said, "you've got it. We don't care about the fireworks." Then she flashed a look at Luke. "Thanks for bringing her in."

"You're welcome, Mrs. Perkins." He didn't read any friendliness in her expression. But he didn't see open hostility, either. She'd apparently decided to stay neutral for now. Luke thought that was eminently fair.

They continued to the table on the far side of the diner. Edgar ended his conversation with Jack and walked over to gather Naomi in his arms. "We're on your side, sweetheart," he murmured.

After he released her, he turned to Luke. "So." He stuck out his hand and Luke shook it. "I know we've met before, Luke, but I can't seem to remember where you're from."

"Most recently from Sacramento, Mr. Perkins. I worked with Nash Bledsoe over there."

"Oh, right. I did hear that." From behind his wire-rimmed glasses, Edgar continued to scrutinize Luke as if wanting to ask more personal questions but hesitating to start in, considering the circumstances. "We'll have to talk later," he said finally.

"I look forward to that." What a whopper that was. Luke doubted that a heart-to-heart with Naomi's dad would go well.

By the time Edgar headed back into the kitchen, Naomi had already taken one of the two remaining chairs, which were at opposite ends of the table. She'd chosen to sit with Emmett on one side of her and Nick Chance on the other.

Luke didn't blame her. He'd gladly take the other end and be the one closest to Clifford Mason, who was dressed in a bloodred shirt with silver piping.

Mason spoke first. "I know who you are, young lady, but I don't believe I know the person you came with. Or why he's here."

Luke's jaw tightened. He didn't care for the tone or the implication. The guy had better watch himself.

"Luke's my research assistant," Naomi said smoothly. "He's here on behalf of the eagles."

Clifford glanced over at Luke, and Luke gave a nod of acknowledgment. He *was* a research assistant…sort of.

Pam Mulholland leaned forward. "Naomi, Emmett has related some very disturbing news regarding our fireworks display. Could you clarify the situation?"

"Certainly." Naomi switched on her laptop. "These pictures were taken yesterday, so the nestlings haven't changed much in twenty-four hours. I wanted you all to see them." She handed the laptop to Emmett. "If you'll pass that around, everyone can get a look at what we need to protect."

Luke had seen the picture. Naomi hadn't had much time to choose one, but she'd found a charmer. The baby eagles looked bright-eyed but vulnerable while their mother perched on the edge of the gigantic nest and gazed down at them. Luke would have liked to say she gazed at them fondly, but an eagle couldn't look fond if it tried. She was imposing, though, and a preview of what those babies could become if allowed to grow up.

Everyone else's food arrived as the laptop circled the table, so there was some juggling involved. Luke didn't have food yet, so he was free to watch all the reactions to the picture.

Emmett chuckled and Pam's expression softened. Mason looked pissed—no surprise there. Jack grinned as if he were personally responsible for those nestlings looking so adorable. Tyler studied them closely, and she too seemed caught by the winsome image.

Nick studied them even more closely than Tyler. "They look healthy to me. Perfectly viable."

Then Luke realized that Nick might be here in his capacity as a vet more than for his aunt Pam. In practical terms, if the nestlings hadn't seemed healthy, then protecting them from fireworks wouldn't have made economic sense.

A waitress came for Naomi's order and she shook her head. Luke caught that and decided he wouldn't get any food, either. He probably couldn't stomach a meal right now anyway. They could eat a late breakfast at the campsite before he went back to work.

Once the laptop had made the rounds, Naomi described the proximity of the nest to the town. "A constant barrage of explosions at close range could easily scare away those parents, leaving the babies to starve. There have been documented cases of that happening, and I can supply that evidence before the end of the day, if you need it."

Mason leaned back in his chair. "Please do. We need a lot more evidence. I find this hard to believe, frankly. Aren't wild creatures supposed to defend their young fiercely? Why abandon them at the first hint of trouble?"

"Not all wild creatures respond the same to a perceived threat," Naomi said. "Some parents defend their young, and others abandon them. Eagles tend to leave."

"You say they *tend* to leave." Mason glared at her. "And you're proposing we cancel a major civic event, one that will bring much-needed revenue into this community, on the *supposition* that two little eagles *might* be harmed. That's a lot of variables. I don't buy the argument."

"I'll have statistics available later today," Naomi said. "Personally, I can't imagine going ahead with a fireworks display if there's even a slight chance that two of our valuable eagles will die as a result."

Mason sent Tyler a challenging glance. "How about you, Mrs. Keller? Are you ready to have all your hard work go down the drain on the slight chance it will cause harm to a couple of eagle chicks?"

"Naturally I would rather we go ahead as planned," Tyler said. "We've put in a lot of work. But this area is dedicated to honoring and protecting its wildlife. To ignore that doesn't feel right."

Jack cleared his throat. "Mr. Mason, have you considered the potential PR nightmare if word gets out that a fireworks display provided by your company caused the death of baby eagles?"

Luke was impressed. Maybe Jack deserved to be in charge of the world after all. The guy had come up with a killer argument.

"Most likely the eagles will be fine," Mason said. "Even if they're not, who will know?"

"Me," Naomi said. "And I will report my findings to Professor Scranton, who's funding this study."

Emmett leaned around Pam, obviously wanting more eye contact with Mason. "I can't say how a college professor might influence the situation, but I can guarantee the influence the Chance family will have. The Last Chance gave permission for the study, and we support Naomi's work. Right, Jack?"

"Yes." Jack's face was like granite. "We certainly do."

Emmett's blue eyes grew very cold. "Just some friendly advice, Mason. When in Jackson Hole, don't mess with the Chances."

Mason laughed. "What do we have here, a gunfight at the O.K. Corral? Give me a break. I have a contract that says I'm supplying fireworks to this event. Cancel the contract and I'll have you all in court."

Pam Mulholland turned to him. "That's enough, Clifford."

He blinked. "Pam? Surely you're not going to let some silly eagles' nest spoil the town's Fourth of July celebration. We're going to put Shoshone on the map, you and I. The townspeople won't be happy about this." He stood and addressed the rest of the diners. "Help me out here, folks. You want your fireworks, right?"

"My kids are counting on it," said one man.

"It'll be good for business," piped up a woman.

Naomi stood, too. "I'm sorry about the last-minute notification, but I've been out at the observation site and just found out about the fireworks. Yes, I'm sure kids will be disappointed, but we're preserving those eagles for their generation. I'll bet if you explained the situation to them, they'd understand. Kids have an affinity for baby creatures."

"So do I." Tyler stood and turned toward the group. "And had I known that fireworks could be a problem for those nesting eagles, I never would have accepted Mr. Mason's offer to provide them."

"I wouldn't have, either." Pam also rose from her

chair. "I own a business, and my guests may be disappointed initially, but not once I explain. Anyone who comes to Shoshone knows it's a haven for wildlife. That's one of the main reasons they visit. Not for fireworks."

Mason glanced at her. "You're missing the point, Pam. There's only a possibility that the eagles will be harmed. To cancel all our careful plans for the *potential* harm to a couple of eagles isn't good business. It's not smart."

Emmett unfolded his lean body from his chair. "Excuse me, Mason." His voice was dangerously low. "But I won't have you taking that tone with the woman I love."

Pam gasped. "Emmett!"

Mason's mouth twisted into a dismissive sneer. "This isn't any of your concern, Sterling. You had your chance. Now it's my turn. Pam and I have a business arrangement. Her emotional response to the eagles is understandable. She's a woman. But once she has a chance to think logically, she'll—"

"Shut up, Mason." Emmett moved Pam gently aside. "Sorry. I know how you hate to make a scene." Then he grabbed Mason by his gaudy red shirt. "I didn't like you when I first laid eyes on you, but I tolerated you because you were a guest in Pam's establishment. Now that you've insulted her by implying that her gender has affected her good judgment, I don't have to tolerate you any longer."

"Pam!" Mason's eyes bulged. "Are you going to let him talk this way?"

"Yes, Clifford, I am. Because you are a horse's ass."

Luke felt like applauding but decided that wasn't appropriate. He did note that both Nick and Jack were smiling.

Emmett continued to hold Mason by his shirtfront. "I'll tell you this once, and once only. Get out of our town. And leave my woman alone." He released his hold, and Mason had to scramble to keep from falling down.

Pam sighed. "Oh, Emmett."

"I'll leave, all right." Mason backed away from the table. "Because you're all *crazy.* Your little town is going to amount to *nothing.* I hope you all rot!" And he ran out of the diner.

Emmett stood there breathing hard, but he didn't seem to know what to do next. Luke considered whether or not to tell him. Emmett had asked him to offer suggestions regarding Pam at any time. This was a critical moment. Even Luke, who avoided entanglements at all costs, recognized it.

He leaned toward Emmett. "Propose, man," he said in an undertone. "Now's the time."

Emmett gulped. Then he squared his shoulders and turned to Pam. "I think you'd better marry me before some other damned fool comes along and thinks you're available, because you're not!"

Pam laughed and threw her arms around his neck. "Finally!" Then, still holding on to a very red Emmett, she glanced at the other customers. "I have witnesses, right? He asked me, and I accepted!"

"We'll back you up, Pam!" shouted someone in the far corner of the room.

"You waited long enough!" cried another.

"This is better than fireworks!" yelled a third person.

Pam gave Emmett a quick kiss before grabbing his hand. "Let's get out of here."

"Hell, yes. This is a nightmare." Blushing furiously, Emmett allowed himself to be led from the diner amid laughter and cheers.

Luke sought Naomi's gaze and they exchanged smiles of triumph. But he detected something else in her expression, an emotion that put him on alert. She seemed…wistful.

He shouldn't be surprised. She wanted a happily-ever-after someday, too. She'd admitted as much. So naturally, when she watched a man declare his love for a woman, she had to start thinking about when that might happen for her.

And here he was, enjoying all the privileges of a potential life mate, without any intention of filling that role. He felt like a poseur, a selfish bastard who was taking the place of someone who could promise to love and cherish her forever.

Then she looked away with an abruptness that made him wonder if she'd been able to guess his thoughts. They'd been together so much lately she might be capable of doing that. He didn't want to hurt her, but he had the horrible suspicion that he wouldn't be able to stop that from happening.

NAOMI TRIED TO talk Luke out of taking her back to the observation site, but he insisted. Arguing with him about it while everyone filed out of the diner wouldn't have been classy, especially because so many people stopped to thank her for protecting the eagles.

So she climbed on behind him as she had before, attracting more attention in the process. She ended up introducing Luke to several people who'd never met him, so getting out of Shoshone took some time.

Finally they reached the outskirts of town. "Thank you for being there," she said.

"I didn't do much. You handled everything beautifully."

"I didn't have to do much, either. Mostly I let Clifford Mason dig himself into a hole. I think if Emmett hadn't grabbed him by the shirt, someone else would have."

"Like one of the Chance brothers?"

"Or others sitting in the diner. Pam is well liked. She runs a quality bed-and-breakfast that's a credit to the town, and she's generous with her money. People don't forget things like someone buying new Christmas decorations for Main Street or having the Shoshone welcome sign repainted. Any man insulting her is creating a problem for himself."

Luke chuckled. "I think he figured that out. His talk about lawsuits faded fast."

"I spoke briefly with Jack, and they've had the guy investigated. He's a shady character, so I think the lawsuit was an empty threat. He might have thought he was dealing with a bunch of hicks who wouldn't know any better."

"Then he didn't do his research."

"Obviously not." She gave in to the temptation to lay her cheek against his back again. But she couldn't shake the nagging feeling that things had changed between them in some subtle way. Emmett's proposal had touched her, and then she'd made the mistake of gazing at Luke. He'd probably thought she was dreaming about the proposal she'd like to receive someday.

Well, she had been, but that didn't mean she expected Luke to do the honors. Luke had said something to Emmett before that proposal, though, and she was curious. "You made a comment to Emmett after Mason left. What was that all about?"

"I told Emmett to propose."

"I wondered. I could sort of read your lips, and then he turned around and did exactly that, as if he might be following orders."

"If he was ever gonna do it, that was the time."

"Oh, Luke." She allowed herself to hug him just a little bit. "Do you realize how long that proposal has been dangling between them, waiting to be said?"

"Awhile, I guess."

"My mother said it's been years. Pam desperately wanted him, but he couldn't get past her wealth, when he doesn't have a whole lot of money. Your nudge was a good thing, Luke."

"You talked to your mom? When?"

"As everyone was leaving, we grabbed a few minutes." She'd noticed Luke having a conversation with

Nick and Jack, so she'd ducked into the kitchen to say goodbye.

"How about your dad? Did you talk to him, too?"

She heard the note of anxiety. "Briefly. He's glad the eagles are safe." In reality, she hadn't invited a deeper discussion with either of her parents. Earlier today she'd thought that speaking to them about Luke was important. Now she wasn't sure.

Luke was pulling away. She couldn't explain how she knew, but she did. To confess everything to her parents made no sense if her special time with Luke was coming to an end soon.

"So you just talked about the eagles."

"Yes. If you're asking whether I explained our situation to them, the answer is no, I didn't."

"Okay." He didn't ask why, and that was telling.

She fell silent for a while and just soaked up being close to him as Smudge walked along the path with a slow and steady gait. She had the distinct feeling she wouldn't ride like this with him again, so she wanted to get all the pleasure from it that she could. He was such an enigma, this man she'd known so intimately yet in some ways knew not at all.

"Tell me something," she said at last. "If you're convinced that marriage ties a person down, why urge Emmett to propose? It seems as if you'd be the least likely one to do that."

"Because I think it would work for him. He's not a traveler. He likes it fine right here, and he's already tied to the ranch. Being tied to Pam, a woman he clearly loves, isn't adding much to his obligations. He was letting her money get in the way, which was only making both of them more miserable."

"I agree, but I'm still surprised you made the suggestion."

He laughed. "You mean because it's none of my business?"

"Well, yeah."

"The night we came home from the Spirits and Spurs, after he'd danced with Pam, he told me that if I ever had another bright idea about how to deal with her, to let him know. So I had a bright idea today, and I let him know."

Naomi smiled and hugged him again. "Then all I can say is well done. Pam looked as if she was lit from within. And I don't suppose she'll ever know that she has you to thank."

"She won't hear it from me, and unless Emmett's completely clueless, he won't tell her. She needs to believe it was Emmett's idea."

"Yes, she does. No woman wants to think a man had to get cues from the sidelines when he was proposing."

"He probably would have thought of it himself anyway."

"I don't know, Luke. He's been shilly-shallying around for a long time, according to my mother. I'm glad you gave him a push."

"Yeah, me, too. They'll be happy."

Luke was such a puzzle to her. He sat on the sidelines—matchmaking, babysitting other people's children, having brief affairs with women—but he never really got in the game. He saw amazing places, but he made no permanent connections with them. He truly was a drifter in the old-fashioned sense of the word.

And yet she felt the tug of strong emotion whenever they had… She couldn't even say they just had sex, because it was more than that. At least it was for her. In her biased opinion, they made love.

They might not be *in* love, but they made love. They cherished each other in a way that lifted the act above the simple joining of bodies for mutual satisfaction. At least she thought so.

But maybe he didn't think so. No, he did. She'd seen it in his eyes. And after watching that special tenderness in his expression while he loved her, she wondered if he'd be able to walk away without regret this time around.

"You're awfully quiet back there."

"It's peaceful riding along like this." She wasn't about to admit that she'd been wondering whether he would miss her when he left.

"So are you hungry?"

She lifted her head in surprise. "Yes, come to think of it, I am. I wasn't the least bit hungry when we were at the diner, but now I'm starving."

"Me, too. So here's my plan. When we get back to the campsite, we cook up some breakfast."

"I'd like that." She wanted to recapture the cozy atmosphere they'd created when it was just the two of them. He didn't seem threatened by that. But when they were in town, surrounded by people who had conventional expectations of what their relationship might become, that was when she felt him starting to leave her.

"You know what else we need?"

"What?" She hoped he was thinking the same thing she was.

"A victory romp."

"Is that what I think it is?"

"Well, you do it naked."

She hugged him tight. "Then it's exactly what I think it is. And yes, we need that." She had him back again. Maybe not for long, but for now.

14

In town Luke had begun to feel trapped, especially after seeing Naomi's reaction to Emmett's proposal, but the closer they came to Naomi's campsite, the more he relaxed. And the fact was, he loved being with her. It wasn't only the sex, which was fantastic. He just plain liked her.

He'd never met a woman who was so at one with nature that she could completely abandon makeup, skinny-dip in a cold stream and walk around a camp without underwear. He admired her devotion to the eagles and her ability to be alone for long periods of time without freaking out.

As if all that weren't enough, she could imitate Tarzan's yell perfectly. He almost asked her to do it again on the way home, because he had loved hearing it. But Smudge might not appreciate that, so he didn't ask.

Then he realized how he had just thought of the campsite: *home.* He had pictured where they were heading, and in his head he'd called it *home.* Oh, boy. That wasn't good.

Maybe leaving the campsite together and returning together had created that sense of coming home. If so, he wished he hadn't brought up the idea of going into town for the Fourth of July celebration. He'd invited her to the celebration, so he should escort her there, right? That would set up another leaving-and-coming-back scenario, as if they lived together.

He'd never lived with a woman, because he'd wanted to avoid that feeling of domesticity, which could lead to marriage, which could lead to the end of life as he knew it. Apparently he'd kidded himself that coming out to her campsite night after night was different from moving in with someone, because, hey, it was camping. She didn't exactly *live* here. Except she did.

And in a sense, so did he. He'd left his sleeping bag, a personal possession, with her. No, it wasn't the same as if he'd brought clothes and toiletries and his collection of DVDs. But it was more than he'd ever done with any woman.

He had a problem, but it wasn't too late to fix it. It wouldn't be too late until he was so firmly tied down that he didn't feel he could leave. He wasn't to that point yet, so he needed to start planning his exit strategy.

He couldn't leave now, with the Fourth of July celebration coming up, especially since he'd asked her to go with him. But afterward he might just as well go. Better to leave while she was still involved with the eagles so she'd have something to take her mind off him. Maybe she wouldn't miss him all that much, but he had a feeling she might.

He had a feeling he was going to miss her, too, and that was all the more reason to get out of town. Staying would only make things worse for both of them. And summer was a good time to travel and find another great place.

Riding into camp after making that decision was a bittersweet experience, because he really had grown to love spending his nights beside her campfire and in her little tent. He and Naomi had fallen into a routine that seemed to suit them both. That also should have been a warning to him. He was becoming entirely too comfortable here.

"I need to check the eagles before we eat," she said as she dismounted.

"You bet." He gave her a smile and swung down from the saddle. "I'll start the fire and get things going." Then he kissed her, because very soon he wouldn't be able to do that anymore. She tasted so damned good.

He forced himself to end the kiss, resisting the temptation to drag her into the tent for the activity he'd planned for after breakfast. He had to keep his eye on the time. Emmett had given him the morning off, not the whole day.

"Get going, lady." He turned her around and gave her a little push. "Before I forget the plan."

"Okay." She blew him a kiss and jogged down the path to the observation platform.

Fool that he was, he watched her go and felt a lump

form in his throat. Wow, he was in way more trouble than he'd thought if he could get choked up over this woman. Clearing his throat, he turned back to Smudge.

The paint stared at him with his warm brown eyes, and Luke realized he was also going to miss the horse, for God's sake. He'd let himself get attached there, too. For a guy who was supposed to have his head screwed on straight, he seemed to have it right up his own butt.

"Come on, Smudge." He led the paint over to his little plot of grass and dropped the reins to the ground. No point in unsaddling him when Luke would be leaving in an hour or so.

First he unzipped the tent flap and double-checked that there was a condom under his sleeping bag. Soon after that, he had the fire going, coffee brewing and bacon sizzling in a pan. That was the other thing. He'd done more cooking this week than he had in the previous six months. At the Last Chance bunkhouse, the cowhands took turns cooking breakfast and dinner. Lunch took place in the ranch house's big dining room, a tradition that allowed the Chances and their hands to mingle and exchange ranch-related information.

Luke had rotated through bunkhouse kitchen duty with the rest of the guys, but he hadn't put much thought into it. Nothing like the planning he'd done for breakfast and dinner with Naomi. He couldn't complain, though, because he'd enjoyed making meals the old-fashioned way, over a campfire. Naomi's gratitude didn't hurt the situation, either. She'd acted as if he were doing her some huge favor when in reality he was simply having fun.

By the time she returned to the campsite, he'd put the finishing touches on the scrambled eggs by adding a little salsa. Naomi liked them that way. He'd piled a few fresh blueberries on each of their tin plates because he knew she liked those, too.

She walked into camp carrying the stool. That had become part of the routine, too. Now he took the flat rock and she took the stool.

"This looks so good!" She gave him a quick kiss on the cheek as she accepted her full plate and a tin mug of coffee. "I was way too nervous to eat anything at the diner, but that's over and we won!"

"We did." He touched his coffee mug to hers. "Or rather, you did. Congratulations."

"No, *we* did. If you hadn't mentioned the fireworks, I hate to think what would have happened." She sat down on the stool.

"That was dumb luck. I didn't know it was important." He settled on the flat rock. "Jack mentioned the fireworks to me the day he came out with little Archie. I didn't have sense enough to realize you needed to know about them." He dug into his food, which tasted better this morning than it ever had, probably because he knew he might only have one more breakfast with her.

"You couldn't have known the fireworks were an issue unless you'd spent a lot of time studying eagles like I have. Clifford Mason is a jerk, but his attitude is common. Why would anyone assume eagles would abandon their young if they felt threatened?"

"I didn't. I had no idea how fragile the situation is.

They build this big-ass nest, and they're such fierce-looking birds. You'd think they'd hold their ground. Or their sticks."

"Well, they might." She gazed at him. "I screwed up part of the celebration without knowing for sure that they'd abandon the nest. I do feel sad about that."

"Don't." He looked into those blue eyes and wondered how in hell he was going to leave. "Mason wasn't exactly a crook, but he wasn't totally legit, either. No telling whether he would have substituted crummy fireworks for the ones he promised."

"True."

"And you gave Emmett a reason to object to the guy on grounds other than jealousy, which led to a proposal. I'll bet Pam is happy about the way things turned out, and knowing her, she'll figure out a way to make up for the lack of fireworks."

"You're right." She smiled at him. "I thought of something else, too. We know about this nest, but there could be others within range of those fireworks. More than two eagle babies might have been at risk."

"There you go." Luke polished off the last of his breakfast. "You might have saved a bunch of little eagles. The Shoshone eagle population may boom as a result of this day." He sipped his coffee and in the process managed to check out her plate to see if she'd finished her meal.

He'd thought he'd been sneaky about it, but her laughter told him different.

She stood and dumped her plate in the kettle of water they always had available for that purpose. Another routine. They'd created them so effortlessly together that he hadn't seen the net of routine and connection being woven until today.

"Yes, I'm finished," she said. "I take it you're ready to move on to our victory romp?"

"I'm more than ready." He got to his feet and dropped his dishes in the same kettle. He needed to hold her, yearned for it in a way that was also a warning. Sure, he was eager for the sex. But he wanted the closeness more.

She pulled her shirt over her head and tossed it on the stool. "Whoops. Hiking boots." She sat down to take them off.

"Let me." Crossing to her, he dropped to his knees.

"I can do it." She grabbed his hands. "Unlacing and removing hiking boots has got to be the least sexy part of undressing a woman."

"Unless it's me taking off your hiking boots." He shoved his hat back and looked at her. "Let me."

Her voice softened. "All right."

As he leaned over her and untied the laces, his hat kept bumping her knees. Finally he took it off and handed it to her. "Hold this a minute."

"I'll just wear it."

"Be my guest." He glanced up at her just to check it out. He was curious, nothing more. She'd never worn his hat and he wondered how she'd look in it.

Then he went very still. He couldn't explain why, but seeing her looking so cute while wearing his hat flooded his chest with warmth. He had a pretty good idea what that indicated, and it wasn't good news.

"Do I look bad?"

"No." He swallowed. "You look so good it hurts." He didn't know why he'd said that and wasn't even sure he knew what he'd meant by it.

But she seemed to. Cupping his face in both hands, she gazed into his eyes. "I know."

That blasted lump formed in his throat again and he broke eye contact. "Let's get these things off." He'd intended to do it slow and sexy, but that didn't matter anymore. He needed her too much to play seductive games.

Pulling the boots off, he tossed them aside. Then he scooped her up and carried her over to the tent as he kissed everywhere he could reach. They'd established another routine—taking off their clothes before they climbed into the small tent—but he ignored it. He didn't have time for that, either.

Their entrance into the tent wasn't elegant, but he got her in there without landing on top of her and squashing her flat. Then he continued kissing her as he worked her out of her bra, shorts and panties.

There. At last he had her the way he wanted her—all creamy, soft skin exposed; all fascinating dips and crevices, mounds and deliciously slippery places available to his hands, lips and tongue. He covered every last inch of her as she moaned and thrashed beneath him.

He made her come twice and would have gone for a third time, but she clutched his head and dragged him up her moist body until she could look into his eyes.

"You," she said, panting. *"Inside me. Now."*

He was still completely dressed, but a man didn't ignore a command like that. He got his pants pulled down and a condom on in less than twenty seconds. It was as close to "now" as he could manage.

He'd prepared his way quite well. One quick thrust and he was right where she'd asked him to be. Bracing himself above her, he looked into her blue eyes. "Like that?"

"Exactly like that." Breathing hard, she pulled at his shirt and the snaps gave way, popping wildly. "This was supposed to be a two-person victory romp, remember?" She stroked his damp chest.

He rocked forward, cinching them up even tighter. "I've been fully present."

She slid her hands upward and cupped his face again as she'd done before. Her gaze probed his as she drew in a ragged breath. "What's going on with you, Luke?"

He was afraid she saw too much, saw through him. "I just...needed to...touch you, kiss you..." He couldn't explain.

"You're leaving, aren't you?"

His pulse leaped. "I always said that I—"

"Yes, I know. But you're going soon. I can feel it."

No, he couldn't tell her like this. Not when he'd plunged into her warmth, when she'd opened herself to him with such trust. Agony sliced through him and he groaned. "Naomi."

"It's okay, Luke." She laid her finger over his lips. "Don't say anything. Just make love to me."

There was that damned lump again, blocking his throat. He couldn't have spoken if he'd wanted to. So he spoke with his body, instead. Holding her gaze, he began to move.

With deep, steady strokes he told her how much she meant to him. He told her that there would never be another woman like her in his life. She would hold a unique and precious place in his memory. And if he were a different sort of man, he would stay and fulfill all those dreams she kept close to her heart.

Her body responded, as it always had. He doubted she could help it, just as he couldn't. They communicated on a different level when they were locked together like this.

And so she arched beneath him as an orgasm claimed her, but this time she didn't cry out. Instead her eyes welled with tears.

The sight of those tears filled him with despair, but he was no less driven by the pulsing of their bodies than she was. He came because he had no choice. Her response demanded his. His surrender was not much of a gift, but it was all he had to offer.

When the shudders lessened, he lowered his head and kissed away her tears. He'd vowed that he wouldn't hurt her, and he'd failed to keep that vow. He might never forgive himself for that.

He left the tent quietly. She'd told him not to say anything—there wasn't anything he *could* say. He'd intended to stay long enough to be her date for the Fourth of July celebration, but he hadn't even been able to accomplish that. She'd guessed his decision, and he'd never lied to her. He wouldn't lie to her now.

Putting himself to rights didn't take very long. His

hat had fallen to the ground when he'd swept her up in his arms. He picked it up, dusted it off and put it on.

Sometime soon he'd give the hat away and get a new one. He'd never be able to wear it after today, transfixed as he'd been by the sight of her wearing his hat. He'd leave it for her, but she wouldn't want the thing, either. She'd have reminders enough without something like that hanging around.

Thank God he hadn't unsaddled Smudge. He climbed aboard the patient horse and rode away from the campsite. About ten minutes into the ride he remembered his sleeping bag, which was still in her tent. Screw it. He'd never be able to use that sleeping bag without thinking of her, either. She'd probably burn the damned thing, and he couldn't blame her if she did.

The ride back to the ranch seemed to take an eternity, and at every turn in the path, he asked himself if he should ride back and talk to her, comfort her in some way. But what good would that do? The only thing that would comfort her was if he stayed, if he changed his entire way of life and became what she needed.

He knew how that could turn out—attending cookouts with stodgy neighbors instead of heading off on adventures to parts unknown. Maybe his father had done him a favor by rejecting his invitation this morning. Luke had probably needed a reminder as to why he'd chosen this life.

When he reached the ranch at last, he felt as if he'd been traveling for days. The place looked familiar, but strange, too, as if he'd already left it in his mind. No one was around, and he realized they were all up at the main dining room for lunch.

Just as well. He gazed at the huge log house that the Chances had built. The grandfather, Archie, had started with a boxy two-story structure. Over the years, two-story wings had been added on either side, canted out like arms ready to welcome visitors.

Or ensnare them. This Chance family was about as tied to one place as anybody could be. Luke had found a few travelers on the fringes of the clan. Tyler Keller used to be an activities director for a cruise line. She and her husband, Alex, traveled quite a bit because Tyler loved doing that.

And to Luke's surprise, he'd found a couple of fellow travelers in Mary Lou Simms, the ranch cook, and her new husband, a ranch hand who went by the single name of Watkins. Gabe Chance competed in cutting-horse events, so he occasionally went out of state for that.

But other than those folks, nobody at the Last Chance had a burning desire to explore the world. They were content to enjoy what they had right here. Luke agreed it was beautiful, but for him it wouldn't be enough. There were too many other beautiful places, and he couldn't ignore the urge to see them.

Because of that, he'd quite likely broken Naomi's heart, and once Emmett and Jack found out, Luke wouldn't be welcome here anymore. With that concept in mind, he quickly took care of Smudge and turned the brown-and-white paint into the pasture. He didn't linger over the horse any more than he'd lingered in

Naomi's camp. Prolonging the moment of separation was never a good idea.

Packing up the belongings he'd stashed in the bunkhouse took no time at all. He had everything loaded in his old truck before the hands started trickling back from lunch. He accepted their good-natured ribbing about his absence this morning as he waited for Emmett to show up.

Eventually he realized Emmett wasn't coming. When he asked someone, he discovered that Jack had given Emmett the rest of the day off so that he could spend it with Pam. They had a wedding to plan.

That meant Luke would have to deal with Jack. Emmett might have been easier to break the news to, especially after Luke had helped the foreman out during the scene at the diner. However, as a result of that event, Emmett wasn't here.

With a resigned sigh, Luke headed up to the main house. He wasn't sure whether to hope that Jack was or wasn't in. If he was out, Luke could talk to Sarah, who held equal power with her sons in anything to do with the ranch.

But Jack had been the one who'd taken Nash's recommendation and hired Luke. If Emmett, Luke's immediate boss, wasn't available, then Jack was the next logical person to accept his resignation. He was also the one most likely to want to clean Luke's clock for hurting Naomi.

Luke mounted the porch steps. He had to admit the long porch, which stretched the entire front of the house, was a good feature. Rocking chairs lined the porch, but Luke had never sat in one. He supposed it would be a nice enough experience.

Sarah came to the door. Tall and silver-haired, with the regal bearing she'd inherited from her New York model mother, she commanded respect with a glance. "Hi, Luke." She opened the door with a friendly smile and stood back so he could walk in. "I'll bet Naomi's a happy lady now that Clifford Mason has left town and taken his fireworks with him."

"She's very glad about that." Luke could say that much without stretching the truth. "Is Jack around?"

"He's in the office. You know your way." She gestured to an open door on the far right side of the living room area. "Go on in. He's handling some paperwork, so he'll welcome an interruption."

"Thanks." Luke touched the brim of his hat before proceeding through the living room. The massive stone fireplace and leather furniture gave the room an air of permanence. No doubt about it, this house was an anchor—that could be seen as a plus or a minus, depending on a person's viewpoint.

Jack sat behind a battered wooden desk that Luke had heard once belonged to his dad. His hat rested brim up on the edge of the desk, and his hair looked as if he'd been running his fingers through it.

He glanced up when Luke came through the door. "Hi. Have a seat."

Luke decided it was best to do that, so he lowered himself into one of the wooden armchairs positioned in front of the desk. He'd sat in this same chair when he'd interviewed for the job last October.

Jack made some notes on a pad of paper before tossing down the pen. He studied Luke for a moment. "I heard what you said to Emmett at the diner. That was good. I appreciate you stepping in."

"He'd mentioned something a few days ago about being open to suggestions when it came to Pam. So I made one."

"We're all in your debt. The guy needed a push in the right direction. Thanks to Mason and you, he got it."

"I hope they'll be very happy."

"Oh, they will. My mom is one of Pam's best friends, and she'll see to it that everything goes smooth as silk." He leaned back in his chair. "But that's not what you came here to talk about, is it?"

"No." Luke cleared his throat. "I hate to do this on short notice, but—"

"Damn it. You're cutting out, aren't you?"

"Yeah. I'm sorry, Jack. I know you could use more notice than this, but it's time. If you don't want to give me a recommendation as a result, I understand."

"You're a good hand and you'll be missed, but we can manage until we find somebody. I'll give you a recommendation. But all that's beside the point. Does Naomi know you're leaving?"

"Yes."

"How's she taking it?"

Luke just looked at him. There was no good answer to that question.

Jack steepled his fingers. "I see."

"You and Emmett were right all along. I shouldn't

have… Well, she would have been better off if I'd left her alone. But I didn't, so the best I can do now is let her start forgetting about me."

"There's a lot of truth to that. If you're not sticking around, then you might as well leave." Jack stood and held out his hand. "When you get settled, send me your address and I'll mail that recommendation."

"Thanks, Jack." Luke shook his hand. "I thought you'd be ready to take me apart."

Jack's eyes glittered. "I haven't talked to Naomi yet. If she's a basket case, I reserve the right to do just that."

"Then maybe I won't send you my new address." Luke touched the brim of his hat. "Thanks for taking me on last year."

"Yeah, well, I'll say one thing for you."

"What's that?"

"You're one hell of a roper. Now get out of here and don't come back unless you have a ring in your pocket for our mutual friend."

"That's not going to happen. I'm not the marrying kind."

"Then I guess we won't be seeing you around these parts."

"No, you won't. Goodbye, Jack." Luke walked out of the office, through the living room and out to the porch. There he paused to catch his breath. Sometimes leaving a place was easy, and sometimes it was hard. Until now it hadn't been gut-wrenching.

But standing around wouldn't make it easier. Hurrying down the porch steps, he climbed into his truck, closed the door and started the engine. As he drove away, he glanced in the rearview mirror. Yep, that house was definitely an anchor.

15

NAOMI HAD ZERO interest in hiking into town for the Fourth of July celebration, but she'd promised her folks she'd be there. Besides, if she hid out in the woods, everyone would assume that she was devastated by Luke's departure.

Jack had come out to check on her and had confirmed that Luke was gone. She'd put on a brave face then, and she'd do the same today. Even though she ached as she'd never ached before, she'd keep that fact to herself.

She'd hiked in very early so she'd be able to shower and change clothes at her parents' house before the parade. She walked in through the kitchen door, as she usually did, and came face-to-face with the one person in the world who could always see right through her.

Her mother stood in front of the stove frying up eggs and bacon, but she put down her spatula and turned when Naomi came in.

"Hi, Mom!" Naomi pasted on the biggest, fakest smile she could manage. "Did you make enough for me?"

"Of course." Her gaze met Naomi's.

And just like that, the charade was over. Naomi's resolve to be tough was no match for the warmth and understanding in her mother's blue eyes. Leaving the backpack by the kitchen table, Naomi went straight into those comforting arms.

"I'm so sorry." Madge Perkins was a small woman, but she had the biggest hug in the world. "I know you cared for him."

Naomi sniffed. "Yeah, I did. But he wasn't right for me."

"No, he wasn't."

"And I'm well rid of him." Naomi didn't believe that, but maybe saying it would start the healing process.

"You most certainly are. You can do much better than him."

"Right." Naomi gave her a quick squeeze and stepped back. "He's last week's news. We have a Fourth of July to celebrate."

Her mom's smile was filled with pride and encouragement. "That's my girl."

"Is everybody okay with not having fireworks?" That was the other reason Naomi hadn't been eager to show up today, in case some folks continued to be upset.

"Absolutely. Pam's subsidizing Lucy over at Lickity Split so Lucy can give away free ice cream all day."

"Oh, good." Some of the tension eased from her

shoulders. "Everyone will love that, and Lucy gets the revenue instead of that creep Mason. I—"

"Hey, has my favorite wildlife expert arrived?" Her father walked into the kitchen wearing a Western shirt with pinstripes of red, white and blue.

"Hey, Dad!" She gave him a hug. "Love the shirt. You're stylin'."

He glanced down at his shirt and smoothed the front pockets. "Just so I don't look too much like that Mason fellow."

"Not a chance. This is way too subtle to be in the Clifford Mason category."

"Well, good, because your mother bought it at some fancy-dancy store in Jackson and wouldn't tell me what she paid for it, which means it's probably the most expensive shirt I've ever owned."

Naomi gave him a thumbs-up. "It looks great on you."

"Thanks." He peered at her through his wire-rimmed glasses. "Are you okay?"

"I'm fine, Dad." It was a forgivable lie. She wasn't going to tell him how much she hurt, because there wasn't a damned thing he could do about it. "All set for the watermelon-eating contest?"

"You know it." He seemed relieved at the change of subject. The contest was the Shoshone Diner's traditional contribution to the festivities, and her father loved it. So did the participants. The Chance boys had multiple wins to their credit.

"I think you should enter this year," her father said.

"Nope." They'd had this discussion in years past,

so she was surprised he'd bring it up again. "Not when you're the judge. It would look bad if I won, and I might. I'm pretty good at eating watermelon."

"So I'll get somebody else to judge."

Both Naomi and her mother stared at him. He'd never offered to give up his cherished role as judge. Then Naomi figured out why he would now.

He wanted her to be so immersed in the activities that she forgot her broken heart. In his mind, a watermelon-eating contest served that purpose like no other. That was both touching and incredibly cute.

Resting her hands on his shoulders, she stood on tiptoes to kiss his cheek. "That's the sweetest thing you've ever offered to do for me. But I'm not robbing you of something you love so much."

"Seriously, I could get Ronald Hutchinson to judge. He'd do it. He knows my watermelon-eating contest is way more fun than his sack race."

"No, Dad." She patted his shoulder. "But if you want to partner up with me and reclaim our title in the sack race, I'm your girl."

"Hey, that sounds great." He grinned at her. "It's good to have you back, kiddo, at least for the summer."

"I love it here. It's my favorite place in the world." The words created an unwelcome reminder of Luke and their recent discussion about favorite places. As she thought about that discussion, her feelings toward him began to shift. Slowly, the deep sorrow that had threatened to drown her began to evaporate in the heat of her growing anger.

Two days ago Luke had claimed that the Jackson

Hole area ranked as one of his favorite places. Yet he'd left. Working at the Last Chance was a dream job for any cowboy, and through Nash, Luke had been lucky enough to land a position there. Yet he'd left.

More than once he'd said how much he enjoyed being with her. Even without the words, she'd known just by looking in his eyes. He had strong feelings for her, perhaps stronger than he'd had for any other woman. Yet he'd left.

Well, good riddance! If he couldn't appreciate that both she and this place were wonderful beyond belief, she was glad that he was gone. He was officially an idiot.

LUKE WAS A certified moron. He surveyed a panorama of snowy peaks, shadowed valleys and a denim-blue lake in the fading light of evening. He'd always wanted to visit Glacier National Park but had never made it. So here he was atop Apgar Mountain with a bucket list–worthy view of the park—its North Fork, to be more precise—but could he enjoy the splendor of the scenery? No, he could not. Oh, he'd tried. He'd told himself that this landscape was spectacular, that it rivaled the Grand Tetons. Even better, he was once more on his own, free to stay here until he grew tired of the place or until his money ran out, whichever came first.

He'd been in the park for three days, hoping that he'd snap out of the funk he was in and get back to his normal travel routine. He'd hiked the impressive trails, all the while congratulating himself on what a great life he had because he was so free of entanglements.

So far he hadn't been able to swallow a single line of that bullshit. In his heart, a place he'd avoided going for years, he knew why he wasn't having any fun. Naomi wasn't here.

And she needed to be here, damn it. There were critters *everywhere.* Deer, bears, raccoons, wolves, birds galore—specifically eagles. Oh, my God, she'd go nuts over the eagles.

Finally, here on this mountain, he faced facts. When he'd met Naomi Perkins, his life had changed forever, and it was never changing back. He'd only put about five hundred miles between them, but even five thousand wouldn't matter. He'd still feel that magnetic pull, still see her face in his dreams, still…love her.

Because he was a moron, he hadn't figured out that he loved her until now, after he'd broken her heart. He knew for a fact he'd smashed it to smithereens. He'd seen it in her eyes when she realized he'd moved up his departure by a couple of months.

He'd seen the misery he was inflicting and he'd left anyway. If he were in her shoes, he wouldn't take him back under any circumstances. A guy who could walk away from Naomi Perkins didn't deserve her.

That was the crux of his dilemma. He didn't deserve her, but if he couldn't have her, he was doomed. She'd shown him that being connected to someone didn't mean being tied down if she was the right someone.

Naomi was the right someone for him. So basically he had no choice but to head back to Shoshone and grovel. It might not work. But it was the only strategy that he'd come up with.

Shoshone was approximately eight hours away, which meant he could be there before dawn the next day. He decided to start driving and hope that a more imaginative approach to winning her back would come to him before he arrived. It didn't. After hours behind the wheel, he still saw groveling as his only option.

He couldn't expect her to respond to that right away, so he could be in for days, weeks, maybe even months of waiting her out and hoping she'd forgive him. That meant he needed his job back, but he'd have to grovel to get that, too. Jack was none too pleased with him.

Then he remembered Jack's final words. Luke wasn't supposed to show his face without a ring in his pocket. Okay, so he'd stop in Jackson and buy a ring. He pulled into town long before the shops opened, so he cruised around the square, located a jewelry store and parked his truck.

He must have dozed off, because the next thing he knew, the sun was out and the square was no longer silent. Shops were open, cars drove past and people walked along the sidewalk in front of him.

He got a better look at the jewelry store and decided it looked pricey. Well, okay. He had quite a bit of room on his credit card.

The brunette woman behind the counter gave him a friendly smile, but he didn't miss the quick once-over that told him he probably looked like hell. That made sense. He hadn't shaved since yesterday morning or changed his clothes—he wore rumpled jeans, hiking boots and a faded plaid shirt.

"May I help you with something?" she asked in a pleasant voice.

"I need a ring." Then he realized that wasn't specific enough. The glass cases glittered with what might be hundreds of rings. "An engagement ring."

Her gaze softened. "Are you interested in a diamond ring or something less traditional?"

"I don't know." He thought about it. "A diamond," he said finally. He figured he couldn't go wrong with a diamond, but if he ventured into that "something less traditional" area, he could get into trouble fast.

"That narrows it down a little. We have solitaires, of course, and then there are the clusters, with a central diamond in the center and smaller ones arranged around it."

"A solitaire. She's not a fussy woman. She'd appreciate simplicity."

"Then let me show you a few and see what you think she might like." The saleswoman laid a couple of trays on top of the case.

The diamonds sparkled under the high-intensity lamps and Luke blinked. He should have had a cup of coffee before coming in here. And maybe some food. He couldn't remember the last time he'd eaten.

"Do you think she'd prefer an emerald cut? Or perhaps a pear shape. Then we have—"

"That one." Luke pointed to a ring with a roundish stone that seemed to shoot fire. "She'd like that."

"You have very good taste." The woman plucked the ring from its slot and held it out.

Luke took the ring between his thumb and forefinger, and his heart began to pound. He was buying a diamond engagement ring. He also was buying it for someone who might never accept it. "Do you have a return policy?"

"Of course." She didn't hesitate. "The choice of a ring is so personal. Couples often come in together. After all, this is something she plans to wear for the rest of her life. You want her to love it."

Luke began to hyperventilate. Until now he'd only thought about getting back in Naomi's good graces. Jack had been the one who'd said a ring was necessary to the process.

"Do you want to think about this?" The woman sounded sympathetic.

"Just for a minute."

"Take your time."

Luke stared at the ring. Soft music played in the background. He hadn't been aware of it before now, but as he listened, he wondered what kind of tunes Naomi liked. Country-and-western probably, but what else?

Did she like to sing? He knew she could yell like Tarzan, but he didn't know if she could sing. Or whistle. He yearned to know every detail about her, big or small.

That would take a long time…years. A lifetime. And when he thought of growing old with Naomi, warmth filled him.

He cleared his throat. "I'll take it."

"All right."

He started to hand it back, and that was the moment he noticed the little white tag fluttering from the band.

He glanced at it and gasped. He'd had no idea. Not a clue. But why would he? He'd never shopped for a diamond ring before.

"Is there a problem?"

He took a shaky breath and handed over the ring. "No. This is the one I want." Reaching in his back pocket, he pulled out his wallet and extracted his credit card. He needed to get his old job back. Immediately.

NAOMI PULLED AN energy drink out of her cooler and unscrewed the cap. The eagle parents had finished feeding their growing nestlings, so she could take a lunch break. Moving the camp stool next to the tree trunk, she sat down and leaned back while she sipped her drink.

Moments like this were dangerous because it was way too easy to think about Luke. If she'd known he'd leave so abruptly, she might not have allowed him to invade her observation post, because now it was filled with vivid memories she couldn't seem to stamp out.

But she hadn't known, and to be fair, neither had he. He hadn't realized their relationship would get so hot so fast. She'd scared him to death, no doubt. She closed her eyes and gave in to the temptation to remember.

She replayed it all—the first day when she'd spilled this green drink all over him, the day when he'd galloped toward her like a Hollywood cowboy and all the days and nights after that. She thought about the way he'd complained about the cold water in the stream, and how much fun they'd had cooking meals together, and sharing the tent, and…

The sound of hoofbeats roused her. Damn. Both Jack and Emmett were worried about her. It would be just like one of them to come up with an excuse to ride out here and see how she was doing.

Sighing, she stood and walked over to the edge of the platform. And there, about a hundred yards away and riding toward her at a brisk trot, was none other than Luke Griffin. Setting down her energy drink, she rubbed her eyes and looked again.

Nope, still seemed like him. Same horse, same broad shoulders and narrow hips. Same tilt of the hat and casual grace in the saddle.

Her heart began to race, and she forced herself to take deep, calming breaths. If he thought he could come out here and make up with her, then leave again when he felt threatened by his feelings, he could forget that noise. She didn't plan to go through that ever again.

Frankly, she was disappointed in whoever had loaned him Smudge after the way he'd left everybody in the lurch, including her. Was he that charming? Could he really make them forget his past sins? Well, *she* wasn't going to forget.

She didn't care if he'd wangled his old job back and planned to spend a few more months here after all. He wouldn't get the time of day from her. She almost wished she had a shotgun so she could point it at him and tell him to back off. Bear spray wouldn't have the same dramatic effect; besides, she'd left it in her tent.

Because she didn't have a shotgun, and because she had no intention of letting him come up on this platform, she ran over to the ladder and pulled the whole thing up. Now she was protected from whatever scheme he had in mind.

Then she returned to the front of the platform and waited, arms crossed. She could tell when he spotted her there, because he slowed Smudge to a walk. About ten yards out, he stopped completely and gazed up at her.

She wished he didn't look so damned gorgeous with his manly physique and freshly shaven jaw. He always had looked like a fantasy and probably always would. That was what he did—traveled around making women salivate. He was very good at it.

She waited for him to speak first. He knew why he was here. She could only suspect, and what she suspected didn't bode well for him.

He rested his hands on the saddle horn. "You seem upset."

"I'm not upset. Just determined."

"About what?"

"That you aren't going to run me around the mulberry bush the way you did before. I've pulled up the ladder."

The irritating man actually laughed. "Good for you. I deserve that, and more."

"What are you doing here?"

"I came to see you."

"That's obvious. But if you came here expecting me to be the same willing wench you left, think again, cowboy."

"I came expecting exactly what I've found, a woman who's furious with me because I ran out on her."

She shrugged and tried for nonchalance. "Don't flatter yourself. I'm over you."

He sighed. "I can't say the same."

"Sweet-talk me all you want. It won't do you a damned bit of good."

Pushing his hat back with his thumb, he gazed up at her. "I haven't treated you the way you should be treated, Naomi, and I readily admit that. But have I ever lied to you?"

She thought about it. No, he hadn't lied. Instead he'd been brutally honest about his drifter lifestyle. She'd known he would leave. She just hadn't expected him to leave so soon.

"No," she said. "I suppose you haven't lied to me."

"In that case, you should be able to take me at my word."

She wasn't sure where this was leading. "I suppose."

"Then here's the deal. I've discovered that life without you is not much fun."

"What?" She stared at him, not comprehending.

"I came back because for the first time I can remember, I'd rather be with someone, with *you,* than be alone. After the way I've treated you, I don't deserve to be welcomed with open arms. But I…I'm planning to stick around and see if I can change that."

She had difficulty forming words. She wondered if this was some sort of hallucination brought about by too many days out here by herself. But the horse snorted and pawed the ground. Birds chirped in the trees, and not far away the stream gurgled over a bed of rocks.

Then a shadow passed overhead, and she looked up as the female eagle returned to the nest. This was real. She was standing on the platform and Luke had just claimed that he preferred being with her to traveling through life alone.

"She's returned to the nest," he said. "So you need to go back to work. I'll leave you to it. See you around." He wheeled Smudge around and started back the way he'd come.

"Wait! You can't make a speech like that and then leave!"

He turned Smudge to face her. "I figure you need time to think about what I've said. I don't want to push you."

Her breath caught. "Push me toward what?"

"Me," he said simply. "I've hurt you. I can't expect to come waltzing back into your life and have you believe that I want to stay."

"Do you?" She began to tremble.

"Yes. I do. Here in this place, but if you have to move for your job, then I'll go there. I want to be with you, Naomi."

As she held his gaze, Smudge walked steadily closer. She gulped in air. "What are you saying, Luke?"

"I love you."

She thought her heart would beat itself right out of her chest. "You…love me?"

"With all my heart. My wild, crazy heart."

"I'll let down the ladder." She whirled around but her foot caught something solid. In that moment she knew what it was. "Watch out!"

But it was too late.

"Aah, shit!" Luke sputtered and cursed.

"I'm coming down!" She dropped the ladder and scrambled to the bottom as fast as she could. By the time she rounded the tree, Luke had dismounted. He'd taken off his hat and was wiping his dripping face with his sleeve.

"I'm so sorry." She ran over to him. "I'm so, so—oof!" The breath left her lungs as he grabbed her and pulled her hard against his chest.

"Don't be sorry." He held her tight. "Just kiss me."

So she did, until both of them were so sticky that she wondered if they'd be glued together for eternity. And that was fine with her.

At last he got them unstuck so he could look into her eyes. "Naomi, I've been a complete fool, but I'll make it up to you, I swear."

She smiled. "You've made a good start."

"I have more than a start. I have a ring in my pocket. I know that was extremely optimistic of me, but I—"

"A *ring?*" She stared at him. "Who are you and what have you done with Luke Griffin?"

His dark eyes clouded. "You don't want it."

"I didn't say that. It's just…you're not the type—and you said…"

"I wasn't the type. But that's because I believed a bunch of junk that wasn't true, and I'd never met you. I'm probably doing this wrong, and I can't get the ring out now because I'm all sticky, but…will you marry me?"

She looked into his eyes and realized he actually

wasn't sure how she'd answer. That was touching. "I'd love to."

The air whooshed out of his lungs. "Oh, thank God. I thought this would take weeks."

"You were prepared to wait weeks for my answer?" She was stunned.

"I was prepared to wait for as long as I had to, but I was determined to make you love me."

"And here I've loved you all along. But I couldn't let you know until…"

"Until I stopped being a damned fool?"

She laughed. "Exactly." And she pulled him into another very sticky kiss. It was the sort of kiss that could last a long, long time…maybe even an eternity.

Epilogue

MICHAEL JAMES HARTFORD was screwed. Putting down his cell phone, he wandered to the window and stared out at the green swath of Central Park five stories below. As Western writer Jim Ford, he'd portrayed himself as a genuine, gold-plated cowboy. His readers believed it, his agent believed it and his editor believed it.

For some reason they'd never questioned why a real cowboy would choose to live in New York City. His books were so authentic that everyone had assumed he owned a secluded ranch where he spent a great deal of time. They'd assumed he could ride and rope and shoot.

He'd let them make those assumptions because the truth—that he belonged to a wealthy New York family and had never been on a horse in his life—wouldn't sell books. Although he didn't need the money from those sales, he needed the satisfaction of being read. He also needed the joy of living in the fantasy world he created every time he wrote a new story.

He'd been caught in a web of his own making. The

books had done so well that he'd become a minor celebrity, which had aroused the interest of his publisher's PR department. They wanted to push him to the next level.

As part of that campaign, they'd scheduled a video of Jim Ford doing all those cowboy things he wrote about. All those things he couldn't do. And they wanted to shoot the video at the end of the month.

Michael had to think of a solution, and he had to think fast. He could fake an injury, but that seemed like the cowardly way out. He'd always meant to visit a dude ranch and learn some of those skills, but deadlines had kept him busy.

The dude ranch still seemed like a good solution, but he'd become so well-known that he couldn't book a week just anywhere and admit that he didn't know how to ride. He required discretion. As he racked his brain for people who might have a ranching connection, he remembered Bethany Grace.

He'd appeared with the motivational author on Opal Knightly's talk show a few months ago, and while they'd hung out in the greenroom, she'd mentioned growing up in Jackson Hole, Wyoming. They'd hit it off so well that they'd exchanged phone numbers. On impulse he scrolled through his contact list and dialed her number.

She answered on the second ring. "Jim! Wow, it's lucky that you called! I'm going to deactivate this number next week."

"How come?" Last he'd heard, she was on the fast

track to becoming a permanent guest on Opal's show, which was a terrific career move.

"I'm getting married and moving to Jackson Hole."

"No kidding? Hey, congratulations. But what about—?"

"I know. Opal's show. I'm not cut out for that, and thanks to various circumstances, I've realized it. So what's up with you? Your books are doing great!"

"They are, and that's why I called you. My publisher wants a video of me being a cowboy, and my skills are…rusty." He winced at that whopper. "I wondered if you know anyone out in Wyoming who would help me on the QT."

"I sure do. I'd work with you myself, but between the televised wedding and leaving on a honeymoon afterward, I'm going crazy."

Michael chuckled. "Opal's making you get hitched on TV?"

"She is, but I can't begrudge her that after the gracious way she's let me out of my contractual obligations. Listen, call Jack Chance at the Last Chance Ranch. Tell him what you need and that I recommended him for the job."

"And he'll be discreet?"

"I guarantee it. The Chance family is a classy bunch. You'll love them all. Let me give you the number."

Michael grabbed a notepad and jotted down Jack Chance's contact info. "Thanks, Bethany. This could save my life—my writing life, at least."

"I just thought of something, though. Jack's mother, Sarah, is getting married soon. Call right away so you can sneak in there and get the job done before the festivities start."

"Don't worry. I'll call the minute I hang up. But back to your marriage. Who's the lucky guy?"

"Nash Bledsoe. He owns a ranch that borders the Last Chance."

Michael heard the love vibrating in her voice as she said that. "He must be special."

"He is."

"I wish you the best, Bethany. I'll admit I'm a little envious." Living a double life, he was caught between two realities—his family's glittery world of charity balls and gallery openings, and the writing community he loved but didn't allow himself to embrace. He didn't belong in either group, which meant he was sometimes lonely.

"You sound a little wistful, Jim. Is everything okay?"

"Sure. I'm fine."

"Well, the Last Chance will do you good. Take it from me, that place has a way of reordering your priorities."

"Right now my priority is getting comfortable on a horse."

Bethany laughed. "I thought I knew what I wanted when I went out there, too. And now look at me. My life is taking off in a totally different direction."

"I doubt that will happen. In fact, I don't want that to happen."

"If you say so. But let's keep in touch. I'm curious to know how this turns out."

"I'll fill you in when you get back from your honeymoon."

"You'd better, or I'll have to rely on Jack's version."

"Then I'll definitely be in touch. And congratulations." As Michael disconnected the call and keyed in Jack Chance's number, he remembered what she'd said about how the Jackson Hole area had affected her. But he didn't need his priorities rearranged. All he needed was riding lessons.

* * * * *

COMING NEXT MONTH FROM

Available July 23, 2013

#759 THE HEART WON'T LIE • *Sons of Chance*
by Vicki Lewis Thompson

Western writer Michael James Hartford needs to learn how to act like a cowboy—fast. But it isn't until he comes to the Last Chance Ranch—and falls for socialite-turned-housekeeper Keri Fitzgerald—that he really discovers how to ride....

#760 TO THE LIMIT • *Uniformly Hot!*
by Jo Leigh

Air force pilot Sam Brody has had his wings clipped. Now he's only teaching other flyboys. And his fling with the hottest woman on the base has taken a nosedive, too...because Emma Lockwood belongs to someone else.

#761 HALF-HITCHED • *The Wrong Bed*
by Isabel Sharpe

Attending a destination wedding is the *perfect* time for Addie Sewell to seduce Kevin, The One Who Got Away. But when she climbs into the wrong bed and discovers sexy yacht owner Derek, The One Who's Here Right Now might just be the ticket!

#762 TAKING HIM DOWN
by Meg Maguire

Rising MMA star Rich Estrada loves exactly two things—his family and a good scrap. But when sexy Lindsey Tuttle works her way into his heart, keeping his priorities straight may just prove the toughest fight of his life.

SPECIAL EXCERPT FROM

Enjoy this sneak peek at

Half-Hitched

by Isabel Sharpe, part of The Wrong Bed series from Harlequin Blaze

Available July 23 wherever Harlequin books are sold.

Addie Sewell held her breath as she headed for Kevin's room. *First bedroom on the right.*

Eleven years later, she'd feel that wonderful mouth on hers again, would feel those strong arms around her, would feel his hand on her breast. And so much more.

Addie reached for the handle and slipped into the room.

Done!

She closed the door carefully behind her, listening for any sign that Kevin had heard her.

He was still, his breathing slow and even.

She was in.

For a few seconds Addie stood quietly, amazed that she'd actually done this, that she, Princess Rut, had snuck mostly naked into a man's room in order to seduce him.

A sudden calm came over her. This was right.

As silently as possible, she walked toward the bed. In the dim light she could see a swathe of naked back, his head bent, partly hidden by the pillow.

A rush of tenderness. Kevin Ames. The One That Got Away.

HBEXP79765

She let her sweater pool at her feet as she pictured Kevin hours earlier. Laughing with that Derek Bates and all the other wedding guests.

Totally naked now, heart pounding, she climbed onto the bed then slid down to spoon behind him. His body was warm against hers, his skin soft, his torso much broader than she'd expected. They fit together perfectly.

She knew the instant he woke up, when his body tensed beside hers.

"It's Addie."

"Addie," he whispered.

Addie smiled. She would have thought after all he had to drink and how soundly he'd been passed out downstairs, that she might have trouble waking him.

She drew her fingers down his powerful arm—strangely bigger than she expected. "Do you mind that I'm here?"

He chuckled, deep and low. Addie stilled. She'd *never* heard Kevin laugh like that.

Before she could think further, his body heaved over and she was underneath him, his broad masculine frame trapping her against the sheets. And before she could say anything, he kissed her, a long, slow sweet kiss.

When he came up for air, she knew she'd have to do something. *Say something.*

But then he was kissing her again. And this time her body caught fire.

Because it was so, so good.

Beyond good. Unbelievably good.

It just wasn't Kevin.